T0278797

The Thankless Foreigner

SEAGULL
BOOKS
•
CELEBRATING
40 YEARS

THE SLOVAK LIST

IRENA BREŽNÁ
The Thankless Foreigner

Translated by Ruth Ahmedzai Kemp

LONDON NEW YORK CALCUTTA

The Slovak List
SERIES EDITOR: Julia Sherwood

LITERÁRNE
INFORMAČNÉ
CENTRUM

swiss arts council
prɔhelvetia

This book has received a subsidy
from SLOLIA Committee, the Centre for
Information on Literature in Bratislava, Slovakia

This publication has been
supported by a grant from
Pro Helvetia, Swiss Arts Council

Seagull Books, 2022

First published in German as *Die undankbare Fremde* by Irena Brežna
Published under the imprint Galiani Berlin
© Verlag Kiepenheuer & Witsch GmbH & Co. KG, Cologne, Germany, 2012

First published in English translation by Seagull Books, 2022
English translation © Ruth Ahmedzai Kemp, 2022

ISBN 978 1 80309 081 8

British Library Cataloguing-in-Publication Data
A catalogue record for this book is available from the British Library

Typeset at Seagull Books, Calcutta, India
Printed and bound in the USA by Integrated Books International

The Thankless Foreigner

We left behind our country, its darkness familiar, and approached the dazzling unknown.

'So much light!' exclaimed Mother, as though that were proof we were heading towards a radiant future. The streetlamps didn't emit a dull, flickering orange like ours, but shone as bright as floodlights. Mother was buzzing with emigration fever; she didn't see the swarms of mosquitoes, midges and moths clinging to the tops of the streetlamps, lured in by the merciless glow, and thrashing about with their little wings and legs, until they were frazzled and fell to the gleaming pavement. And the glaring light of the unknown devoured the stars.

In the barracks we were interrogated by a captain with several speech defects. He couldn't roll his *r* or pronounce any of the letters *ž*, *l'*, *t'*, *dž*, *ň* and *ô*, and he stressed the wrong syllable on our surname, so I hardly recognized myself. Writing it on a form, he stripped off all the hats and wings.

'You don't need all those twiddly bits here.'

He also struck off my rounded, feminine ending, giving me my father and brother's surname. They sat there in silence, passive witnesses to my mutilation. What was I supposed to do with this masculine version, stripped bare? I shivered.

The captain leaned back, satisfied. 'Have you come to seek refuge here because of our freedom of expression?'

We weren't familiar with this long word: *Meinungsäu-ßerungsfreiheit*. Opinion-expression-freedom. Did we have to express our opinions freely to this man, before he would give us all a bed and a blanket? But saying what you think sows only discord, leaves you isolated, locked in solitary confinement.

The captain waited in vain for our opinions, then asked, his voice suspiciously low: 'What is your faith?'

I feared that Mother and Father would seal a pact with the Devil and bring God into play, but they remained godless and said nothing.

Then the man turned to me. 'What do you believe in, young lady?'

'A better world.'

'Then you've come to the right place. Welcome!'

He winked at me and sealed my fate with a stamp.

A gaunt woman led us down long corridors. I was caressed by her pitying eyes. I peered around to see which unfortunate person her look was intended for, but the world was empty. This woman, who had no make-up on and whose hair wasn't backcombed, felt sorry for me! I checked my body;

no, I was all there. I felt my soul limp over to the refugee bed. It was paralysed. That's when we were handed the rough, plaid blankets. The gym hall was full of our compatriots sitting on camp beds. I searched in their eyes for a personal opinion they might want to part with, but I found nothing but dazed moths. When someone joked about the occupation, my lost laugh surfaced, only to then be drowned in tears. I wept over this last joke from our dictatorship. Now we would have to live with democracy and without jokes. Our compatriots spoke of foreign lands, speculating on where they would be better off. We left the plaid blankets behind, still folded, and set off again.

The mad thing about our story was that we had been attacked by our best friends, and now we were stranded in an enemy country after fleeing from our allies' troops. It was midnight before we reached a town. We were given our own room in a hotel full of refugees. We were only allowed to order the cheapest food, but that was no hardship; even the most expensive dishes weren't exactly appetizing. My grandmother's national dishes were dismissed here as unhealthy. They had hard cheese here, but we weren't supposed to talk about it.

'Don't talk cheese,' our language teacher told us. 'Don't talk nonsense.'

That was where I met Mara, a girl from my country. I envied her bra stuffed with cotton wool. She was a good friend and stole one for me, too. After our language lesson, we went to browse the clothes that hung on rails outside on the street, left stranded like foreign girls, vulnerable to theft. Serious-looking, skinny women in crumpled linen trousers, as austere as my new masculine surname, walked past without even a glance at the shiny taffeta miniskirts and the shimmering golden velvet jackets.

'They're not women,' said Mara. 'Or they'd be throwing themselves at these clothes. How sad that nobody wants them.'

After Mara had brought disgrace upon our people, I wrote to her at the juvenile detention centre. 'Dear Mara, it's so unfair that you can't see the sales. The miniskirts have red price tags like blood-shot eyes after crying.'

Mara came back after three weeks instead of three years. The court must have been having a sale on sentences.

The head of the interpreting service reminds her international army of linguistic work-for-hire, 'Just mediate. Don't intervene.'

She isn't suspended in the continental rift; she doesn't know the crash of cultures colliding. Before every assignment I go over the same drill: take care of yourself, leave the banks of the river untouched, don't offer yourself as a bridge that's always there to rely on, or they'll trample all over you and you'll collapse. Be a linguistic ferry. Take your passengers across, set them down, then erase their faces from your memory.

All the same, something from both banks still clings to the ferrywoman. I interpret from three languages. Whenever I have an assignment, I hop on my bike and, against the hum of the wheels, I wonder to myself which country today's passengers will be from. I like that moment when they stand before me and the language is revealed. I often guess the language a few seconds earlier. I can tell which combination of sounds has shaped the mouth. Then I greet the client and the greeting is for the language, too. Languages are living creatures. They live among us, some mooch about, others prance around, clatter, stutter, whisper. We feed and clothe our languages; they might be well fed or malnourished, smart or scruffy. My hearing is heightened when I have a migraine. A vexed, shrill voice slices through my mind, I screw my eyes in pain. If the voice is smooth and soothing, I bathe in it and begin to heal.

The pregnant woman and her husband are sitting in the waiting room of the gynaecology clinic; I recognize the couple from how lost they look. I approach them with a big smile, but their faces tense up. Where they come from, it raises suspicion if you smile in a public space. A smile means you want something. When she lies back on the examination chair and the nurse uses a device to fasten black straps around her stomach, she is shackled to her condition. For days after, I cannot stop picturing this pregnant woman, there before my eyes, with me all the time worrying whether in the throes of labour she will understand the word 'push'. I try to reassure myself. If the midwife barks 'Push!' at her, she'll surely recognize it from the strength of her tone. Then I hear a scream, and her arched belly slumps. At that moment the phone rings. They need me in the delivery room right away.

'The cervix is already dilated to eight centimetres,' the midwife calls to me, then she sends me out again.

In the corridor, on the other side of the solid door, the female doctor quickly runs through some questions with the husband. 'Any deformities, twins or triplets in the family?'

'No.'

'Diabetes? Heart problems?'

'No. No.'

'Does she take drugs? What about alcohol? Does she smoke? Prone to depression?'

'She's healthy,' he says, loudly.

My mind goes blank, I fall silent. This dilating cervix has rendered me speechless. At short intervals we hear screeching like an owl. Suddenly it goes quiet, then we hear a faint whimper.

I throw myself around the husband's neck. 'She did it!'

He raises his arms to the sky. 'May God grant you all your wishes!'

He digs a watermelon out of his backpack and hands it to me. His face is a glowing paper lantern, his cheeks fill like they're pumped up with laughing gas, inflating instead of her stomach into the summer afternoon. On a pedestal in the delivery room, the placenta congeals into mounds of black and red, the young mother lies naked and still, her stomach is broad, her head tilted to one side. The newborn opens its eyes.

I let all my languages go and at home I eat the entire watermelon.

We had stepped into a pre-revolutionary past. The slogans on the walls weren't calling for us to dismantle the strata of society, but instead urged people to lie down on a mattress made of several layers of foam. The respectable-looking man on the billboard who promised 'We'll take care of you' didn't let on that his care had to be bought. A smiling housewife urged us with 'Only the best for you' down on to our knees to polish the kitchen floor.

Mara was outraged. 'Did we leave our country for the sake of the freedom to choose between one toxic cleaning product and another?'

There was no crowd we could blend into, like we used to at the rallies for the glory of the proletariat. Here, there were just two long-haired guys holding a banner that read THE RIGHT TO BE LAZY, taking it seriously like it was a job. Mara and I went to wherever we could find people huddled together happily. But at the cinema there were just a few men. Since the women didn't have the right to vote in this country, they probably didn't go to the movies either. Not that the film was political: two female friends were having coffee and cake in a living room with a man, and when they took off their bras, the audience inched in closer to us. When we got to a sci-fi sequence with the protagonist unbuttoning his trousers, we ran out of there.

'We're not ever accepting an invitation to coffee and cake,' said Mara.

But the only glimpse we had of the private sphere was on posters and billboards. The locals didn't offer foreigners the right to be lazy on their three-piece suites. Instead, you had free entry to one venerable building that looked like a supreme court, a natural history museum and a railway station rolled into one. Here, items were displayed on several floors beneath a glass dome, all with discreet price tags. Mostly useless, but colourful and made of every material imaginable, enthroned majestically under spotlights. Evidence of high culture. Evolution from the primordial through natural selection. The biodiversity, the intermediate species, that resulted from mutation. In our country, everything was the same as when the world was created: just one kind of bread, one lipstick, one mother, one party, one can of fish, and very rarely, one pair of nylon tights.

It would have been cruel to the objects, to choose just one and reject the others. I staggered out, sat on a park bench, and mentally plucked at my jumbled wish list until there was only one item left. Then I forced myself to be blinkered as I went back inside, but even when I tried not to look at the objects, they called out to me. To shop here you had to be deaf and blind. I buckled on a wide belt just before the store closed. I gave the money left over to a man sitting on the pavement, shunned by the objects. His beard was clumpy, his dog was curled up and lifeless beside an empty bowl, like an object, but with no price tag. If homeless people were made of gaudy, glossy plastic, they would be dusted off, touted and coveted until they'd sold out. Their misfortune was to be still alive and not shiny.

Mara said there were places where you could peek inside their houses, like shop windows with women sitting in frilly lingerie and boots. And the men didn't let them out, but just rented them for a while and then put them back on display. And the women didn't run away; they were objectified and stayed put like the objects they had become. And since objects had the majority in a democracy, they held sway, and all the people could do was bow before them and extol their virtues at 9.99 CHF and prices like that. They were as afraid of zeros as they were of the homeless. If you were a zero, you'd be homeless.

The woman sits indoors in this foreign place with her screaming daughter, barely ever taking her out. She's embarrassed of the screaming.

'Were you happy about your daughter when you first you saw her?' the neurologist asks.

'I was relieved.'

'Were you anxious during your pregnancy?'

The woman starts to cry. The doctor apologizes for delving into the past. My voice trundles along evenly in both languages, I'm careful to maintain eye contact, turning my head to the right, to the left. Eye contact is part of the job. More than that, this afternoon it's part of the medical history. The two-year-old has never made long or contented eye contact with her mother.

If during the war it was the occupiers, now in the post-war period it's their own compatriots, the collaborators, who are ambushing houses at dawn, kidnapping people and selling their mutilated corpses to their families. She rarely saw her husband; every night he was somewhere else, sometimes out in the woods, sometimes with relatives. But once, when she was three months pregnant, they captured him, and after five days he was ransomed for the value of ten sheep. She doesn't know what they did to him in their torture chamber. But after that he was a different person. All he wanted was to leave.

At night, smugglers took them across borders, past infrared cameras. Fear twisted her stomach and the foetus pressed against her abdominal wall. In the refugee hostel, the pregnant woman had a breakdown. Lying in the empty hospital room at night in this strange place was like being all alone in the universe. Her blood pressure skyrocketed. She still wasn't full term, but the doctors said the baby needed relief from the pressure.

Her husband meets his fellow countrymen, talks politics, goes to his language lessons. She stays alone in the room with the child. It's hot and humid inside, and she keeps the blinds halfway down during the day, too. She never once screamed, not even when the bombs were falling. Losing your composure is not the done thing. Her daughter carries her mother's suppressed screams into the world, uttering sounds but not words. The mother is silent, thinking of the country she has left behind, her thoughts flowing back there like a drip from a leaking pipe. The daughter can't see the world in its vastness, she was born within the narrow confines of fear. Hers is a confined view of the world.

'An autistic disorder,' came the neurologist's diagnosis a few weeks later.

The father's eyes become a dull yellow, unmoving, his neck sinks into his trunk, his arms go limp. Sweat streams from his forehead, from his hairy forearms. His mind doesn't know what 'autistic' means, but the body senses it and plays dead. Then the words stream out of him. This new calamity reminds him of another, of how he was abducted, beaten around the head with a sack filled with sand, until he signed a statement saying he would obey any command, even to kill. He surrendered then, with the same rigidity as now. He is now blind in one eye and there is constant noise in his head. And the fear is still there. He feels life has punished him, there's no stopping him now, he's complaining about their two-room apartment on the busy street, about the welfare office that is nagging him to find a job.

'I haven't had an education—there was a war on. And I can't get my head around this language.'

The daughter hits the floor with a wooden block, flies into a rage, grimaces and gnashes her teeth. She doesn't see me, I'm a large block that her brain can't process. She is selective and *persistent, obsessively exploring details; she'll never be able to enjoy the spring blossom.*

'She never does what I say. Have we spoiled her?' The mother sighs. Then, worried they might be seen as bad parents who have failed in their duty, she adds, 'We're strict with her, we smack her. That calms her down.'

'Because it's body language,' explains the doctor.

'It's the paediatrician's fault. I asked him, did I have enough milk? He waved it off. My daughter was screaming from hunger.'

'Autism doesn't come from hunger,' the doctor says calmly.

The father disagrees. 'I know what hunger is. Hunger doesn't make you smart.'

After the war, there have been a lot of children born with deformities. They are quickly disposed of in a bucket, and children with Down's syndrome are kept hidden at home. So many anomalies at once. Collateral damage. A disabled child violates the family honour. But in no way does it violate the honour of the culprits.

The mother lifts her daughter up. 'You need to be up there in the conference halls. That's the place for your shouting.'

We moved into a new apartment block on the edge of town. My parents got a job on the twelfth floor of a company that made chemical dyes. Mother was proud that thanks to her the world was becoming more colourful. She took me with her to buy furniture with her first pay packet. We were shown some fancy trash in the cellar of a family house. When the seller named his price, my mother shook her head and tutted. The closer he looked at us, the sadder he became. As if it might make him happier, he lowered his prices. He dropped them so much that Mother just nodded. This man was ashamed of his house and his peaceful life, ashamed of the fact that there was nothing he could do about the injustice that had befallen our country, and was utterly ashamed that Mama was happy with his furniture. As agitated as he was, he remained composed and didn't humiliate us with ridiculously low prices. I didn't know that shame could be so well-meaning, and it was this shame that welcomed us, amid this bourgeois junk in this foreign place. As is the case with any welcoming ceremony, there was also a gift thrown in. When I asked the price of a red kilim, the man gently picked it up from the floor, cradling it like a newborn, and said, 'It's yours.'

He gave it to me without a sigh and without planting a moist kiss on my forehead. And that was how I learned that here good feelings crept about in the shadows, camouflaged and silent like partisans. In the evening I lay down on the kilim and wept. From then on, my tears visited me once a week, I'd open the door for them, and we'd spend the night together. One of those nights I found out that I was rich, I possessed something that the ashamed man didn't have: a tragic fate. It wasn't something I needed to worry about losing, or think about how to maintain its value. A tragic fate was a stable possession. It was people who had known only minor misfortunes who got worked up about trivialities.

There was no threat of shortages here, there was ample supply of washing machines, cars and cleaning products, and Mother was convinced we were happy.

'What's up with you, you grump?' she nagged, exasperated with me. 'Smile for once!'

Since I had lost the broad skin of my community, I wrapped myself tightly in self-pity, burying myself in my resentment towards the unfamiliar. I felt like an object my mother had installed in a strange house, like an underage bride, thrown back a hundred years, married off to a country like an austere old man. I was supposed to love and respect him, get along with him for a lifetime. I had been betrayed in everything that constitutes a human being. Mother hadn't paraded a hundred princes before me, she hadn't asked me, 'Which do you prefer?' or, 'Do you even want to get married?' Instead, she said decisively, 'There's no oppression here.'

For me, my country had meant a playful mother tongue, laughing with my friends, a sense of belonging as a matter of course, a warm current that had swept me along. I'd had gills and all of a sudden I was hurled out onto the riverbank, I could hear my lungs growing, every breath hurt. My brother continued to beat me, as though we didn't now live in a humane society. I moved out.

The world was fragmented into 'me' and 'the foreign country'. I called it 'my husband'. When I looked at 'my husband' I saw what he didn't see. He didn't have a moon face, his face was a grain of wheat, elongated and hard. I couldn't rest in it. It was busy germinating, sprouting, ripening, until the next harvest and the next and the one after that. How did this face sleep? I wanted to take it in my hands and smooth it out, but it scared me. Action hatched directly from his words. If an idea came up, he didn't let it hover in the air, it wasn't a balloon to gaze at; he would straight away grab it, ground it, make plans for it. Time, location, procedure, contingencies. If I was going to make myself at home here, I felt I had to make 'my husband' more like the people I had abandoned who would rather share anecdotes and indulge in dreams than take action. This task loomed before me like the snow-capped peaks that emerge in the distance on a clear day.

The prison van with tinted windows pulls into the courtyard. I go upstairs and in the waiting room I leaf through the tabloid magazines, the only thing with any colour in this establishment. I quickly read a story about a murder until a cheerful policeman appears.

'What sort of case is it?'

'Organized crime. They come here to steal. A free country doesn't mean it's a free-for-all.'

The young defendant staggers in, rolls his eyes, trembles and pulls his sheepskin jacket around his sunken chest.

'I'm cold turkey. Am I going to be released?'

The lawyer looks through the files, his light blue eyes staring wide. His brown curls stand tall in agitation.

'Stealing three perfumes is hardly reason to keep you in prison.'

'I can't take any more—I've got the shakes, my blood pressure's up. Haven't had a hit for two days.'

'How often do you need to take it?'

'Every four or five hours. The heroin's dirty here, it doesn't keep you high for long. It's so pure back home. A gram lasts two weeks.'

It sounds like patriotism. The accused's face has a hazy glow.

When the bell rings, we walk into the courtroom.

'I ask the court and your country for forgiveness. I was led astray, and I promise never to steal again, my word of honour.'

I embellish his words, adding 'honourable court' and 'your wonderful country', and at 'word of honour' my voice stumbles with emotion. The strange pathos arouses suspicion, however. The lawyer is the only one who listens benevolently to the foreign sounds before delivering his fiery defence.

Our interpreting contracts oblige us to reproduce what has been said with scrupulous accuracy. Deliberately falsifying a translation carries a prison sentence of several years. And we're supposed to be punctual and smartly dressed. I'm too dishevelled for this well-groomed vocation. Other people's fates sweep me out to the open sea, the wind tearing at my emotions and thoughts.

In the corridor, the defendant asks if he can smoke.

'We're not that bad,' says the policeman, joining him for a cigarette.

'I hate the dealers,' says the young man. 'There's one who sits at the train station, playing with his tongue—that means, "I've got cocaine." I could break his neck.'

'But that's just an obsessive thought,' I say, trying to be his therapist.

'Well, you need a strong will, but the drug destroys it. I used to be a boxer; I was a hundred kilos. If I don't get out today, it's going to be a bad night without a fix. A lot of people have choked on their own tongues.'

The accused speaks of the drug with respect and loathing, it is his friend and his foe, father and mother, heaven and hell and life itself. He has discovered nothing else within himself besides his body, which he sacrifices to the drug for it to destroy. His contribution to the conversation is to brag about his heroic endurance throughout this destruction.

'His problem is self-loathing,' I note. 'That's what this is about, not prison or being released. How can he learn to love himself?' I muse, but the lawyer impatiently reminds me to just interpret.

'You applied for asylum on the grounds that there's a war in your country. Which war are you referring to?'

'The worst thing is there's a heroin factory there.' The defendant smokes with his eyes closed until the bell rings.

'Four weeks of pre-trial detention, then detention pending deportation, then deportation.'

The judge tries to sound indifferent as he delivers the judgement. The policeman stirs to life and leads the prisoner away.

'The only reason he's been locked up is that he's a foreigner. That's how you criminalize people. Everyone has the right to do what they want with their body,' says the lawyer, fuming. He looks like someone's slapped him, his curly hair lying flat over his ears.

The judge's response is contrite. 'I couldn't let him go. He needs the heroin. It won't be long until he's back in the dock.'

My name no longer belonged to me. People pronounced it with a stutter; it sounded wrong, awkward. A constant reminder that I didn't fit in. And my way of speaking the new language was still suspicious with its crags and fissures. I'd make a mistake; a pothole would open up. The locals wanted everything smoothed out, the potholes concreted over.

'Try to assimilate,' my teacher would coax me. 'Imagine walking down the street and everyone thinking you're from here.'

But I knew my flat moon face would give me away. And so what? I didn't want to stretch it out or put down roots like a grain of wheat.

The meadows were carved up by electric fences, cows grazing behind signs yelling PRIVATE KEEP OUT. I was used to wide-open fields stretching beyond the horizon as far as the death strip. Here, the ponds didn't belong to us all, even the fish were privately owned. Where could I escape the private, and run towards the sun, and scream until I dropped? Emotions that transgressed boundaries were regarded with suspicion, like an attempt to expropriate private property. Remember the fairy tale about the magic porridge pot, which overflowed until the porridge spilled over the kitchen floor, then out of the house, flowing on and on across the country-side? Nobody had heard of it here. The locals preferred horror stories about our rogue regime, which made their eyes turn velvety. They would have liked to take me in their arms, but they didn't dare to. The body was private property behind an invisible iron curtain.

'Here you need a licence before you're even allowed to stroke someone on the cheek,' said Mara.

I wanted to release them from their curse, but whenever I tried to approach someone, they would flinch.

'How terrible life's been to you, you poor thing. You'll be fine now that you're here,' they would say, offering a hand-shake on parting.

There was no washing machine that could wash my old self clean so I could start an impeccable new life. I was sup-posed to be grateful to live here. And always punctual. But why should I be punctually grateful, and to whom, when this better world was working out so badly for me? Home is where you can have a good whinge—and I had no home.

I delivered newspapers early in the morning before school. I would toss them at the doors of the big villas, humming to the rattle of the cart, to the beat of my first job. I was supposed to bend down, lay the newspaper on the doorstep carefully, tread softly and dress inoffensively. After all, I was on the lowest rung of the social ladder, we shouldn't confuse our roles which had evolved over centuries and had stood the test of time, as my boss reminded me. He laughed at his own unrevolutionary words; it was the way of the world, but what could we do? I carried on walking boldly upright at dawn pushing my little cart, with my hair loose, while the residents' complaints about me piled up on the manager's desk.

'Either you tie your hair up, or I'm going to have to let you go.'

I remained resolutely untied up. I let my thick curls flow freely over my shoulders. I combed my hair by the window in the morning, hoping to attract an admiring glance from the street. But instead, someone collected a clump of my hair in the yard below, wrapped it in toilet paper and posted the package into our letterbox. It wasn't my treasured possession, but dirt to be flushed down the toilet. And not a single word in there with it. The light package spoke for itself, the message weighed heavily. The street was oppressively quiet, and the light glinted on the row of neatly tied black rubbish sacks. I imagined myself being disposed of in one. Even freshly fallen leaves were seen as garbage. Voracious, noisy vacuum cleaners cruised around gobbling up the familiar rustle of autumn.

In this permanently vulnerable state, I was on the verge of tears; they fell every time I stumbled. The action of a single person would send me reeling, a cosmic blow. All I wanted was to escape from this neatly swept vacuum where I was told off endlessly, to be back on the pavements of my hometown, strewn with rubbish. Home was where there were familiar signs of life. Here in this foreign place, that stench became the fragrant aroma of home and freedom.

I can tell from her pale complexion and undefined figure that the young woman has already spent weeks in prison. Her thoughts are racing in her motionless body. She has attacks of trembling, and her small blue eyes glisten like a puddle at the bottom of a well. They have cried all that they can. She doesn't understand what she has done wrong; her thoughts keep hitting against a brick wall. She used to clean other people's houses morning to night, she has always been hardworking and law-abiding. When her boyfriend asked her to take some packages to another country, she did it out of the goodness of her heart. Bending forward, she squeezes her hands together, as if trying to wring her heart out too. She wasn't paid for it; she was just glad to help. She would never turn anyone down, especially not her boyfriend after he has been so good to her.

She grew up destitute, and this man helped her get out and bought her exactly the jeans she wanted, without even a glance at the price tag. She had never met anyone like that, a man who was cultured yet reserved. She couldn't quite figure him out. When fifteen policemen stormed the flat three months ago, that was when she realized she was the fiancée of a drug baron. They aimed their guns at her, ready to fire; he had already fled over the hills and far away. She sits there on the plain defendant's chair, rubbing together her sweaty hands.

'I'm happy to help you. Just tell me what you need.'

She's offering herself up to the judge, but he doesn't want anything from her. He remands her in custody for eight more weeks pending investigation.

The policewoman places handcuffs on her.

'How are things in prison?' her lawyer asks.

She grimaces. 'I won't have anything to do with the other woman, the murderer. And what is there to do? Watch TV or watch TV.'

'Do you still love your boyfriend?'

She shakes her head, a fraction too quickly. 'I've lost everything because of him: the flat, my cleaning job—even if it was illegal and badly paid. And now I'm afraid he might get back at me.' She curls up, protectively.

'There's not a single woman I've ever represented who's acted on her own,' the lawyer says to me, pensive. 'Behind every female offender there's a man pulling the strings.'

'Being weak is also a crime,' I say. 'Not speaking up, not finding the strength to change sides, remaining ignorant and obedient out of convenience or fear, not managing to break away from the wrong crowd.'

The man is from an area I know well. We exchange a few names of local people and places, like we're at a family reunion. I am quickly swept along by the current of familiarity, gesticulating wildly, never mind that in this country speaking with your hands suggests non-conformity and lack of control. The lawyer tries to drag me out of the whirlpool back onto his raft: his body stiffens, he speaks in chopped phrases, back-to-back legal terminology like planks nailed together.

The more walls and rules there are, the more I want to be free. The prison is a soiled cloister that inspires crazed hopes. The path trodden by the offender is clear to see. The question is, will he repent? May light fall upon this hour, when we're here because of his deeds, and upon this room with no natural lighting. That is why I'm here, and interpreting is only a pretext.

'I have some news for you. It's not too bad,' says the lawyer in that understated manner they have here. 'You're to be released today.'

The prisoner slowly straightens up, unfurls his clenched fingers, and deftly slips the lawyer's business card into his sock as two wardens step into the room. His dexterity suggests that he's at home behind bars. He praises the prison food: schnitzel on a Sunday and ice cream for dessert. Besides, people treat him with respect and he has everything he needs. Yet sometimes he feels like lashing out, but against what? In custody, it's like everything's made of cotton wool, every decision is taken away from him. As we leave, he stands up straight and looks at us as if deeply moved, with his hand on his heart, as though it were his mother and father forsaking him.

'Is the man innocent?' I ask the lawyer.

'He's been charged with a dozen offences across the conti-nent, but they can't prove anything.'

A warden in a light-blue uniform marches with a broad gait like a sailor down the long corridor and brings the lawyer and me back to the prison entrance. The receptionist wishes us a nice day like a tour guide bidding her guests farewell as they disembark after a Sunday-afternoon boat trip.

The locals approached conversation as if they worked at an information desk: 'When did you get here? Where do you live? Where are you going? And when?'

Some knew entire train and bus timetables off by heart. I was quickly written off as unreliable, unable even to remember the opening hours of the immigration police. Back home, who knew where we were going, or if we had got there yet? We frittered away the time with idle chatter. Here, if I ever attempted to charm them with my wit, it was met with raised eyebrows. Daring to be not only ambiguous but frivolous, too. The teacher explained to us the correct way of making con-versation: 'Outline what you plan to say and for how long, and don't forget to state your aim. That way your interlocutor will feel reassured.' For me, the only thing I could be sure of was the tedium of it all. The teacher demonstrated by explaining at length what he intended to cover in the lesson, before ticking off the topics one by one. I longed for a surprise, and I adored the word itself—*Überraschung*—where things happen so quickly—*überrasch*—like ideas bursting out and interrupting the lesson.

The teacher rejected surprises outright. 'That's not in the plan.'

I gazed into the distance, lacking focus on close detail, and my speech wandered all over the place.

'Just a moment. Everything in the right order,' he would interrupt me, channelling my torrent into rivulets. This way he could understand me better, he declared, satisfied.

I would rush to parties, to gorge myself on the conviviality. But a party was a seamless continuation of work. The guests were informed in writing of both the start time and the intended end time. Conversations revolved around building permits, the election of the president of the civil court and rising medical insurance fees, while Klärli, Vreneli and Lieseli stood around in silence like forgotten umbrellas—after all, females were grammatically neuter here. I didn't come here to hold my tongue. Permissive as the guests were, they granted me limited freedom to speak, but rather than finding my stories captivating, they would hack them apart with practical solutions. They wanted to solve the world, whereas I just wanted to tell it.

If a guest arrived uninvited, they called it an incursion. When planning a military assault on this scale, you were supposed to give at least some advance warning. 'I shall descend on you in three weeks' time'—that was how people tended to threaten a visit. Other methods of ambush were unheard of. With increasingly frayed nerves, the hosts ensured strict compliance with the stipulated conditions. Even children's parties had pre-ordained interludes, patiently rehearsed with the small guests so they knew what to expect. To survive such an over-planned party demanded stamina on the part of the attendees. Neither was it all over when the visitors dispersed. Only now was exuberance permitted: from a safe distance, concealed in an envelope, the guests sent pre-printed thank-you cards gushing with exclamation marks.

Without the slightest clue of what the following day would bring, I was unable to participate in the locals' favourite guessing game: what would the temperature be in the mountains or under the chimney of the factory in the northwest? Would the forecast prove correct? The umbrella was waiting by the door, just in case. I would talk of weather I remembered, where you'd be drenched right through or warmed in an intimately physical way. But here, there were no miracles: the sun followed its path, as reliable as a tax adviser. The rain came on time, as predicted, as punctual as the post. Like the weatherman, the postman was the bearer of news good and bad, every kind of missive passing through his hands. This folk hero would never succumb to the temptation to tear open a thick package like a thunderstorm tears the heavens apart. Invoices didn't burst into flame en route and no one ran off with cash deposits. Discipline, fought for and staunchly defended for centuries, was a tangible benefit. It was just a shame that neither the bus conductors nor the postmen were trained to exchange a few non-functional words in passing.

But telling stories wasn't the locals' strong suit in any case. Talented storytellers don't stick so closely to the facts. And what tragedies did they have to pay tribute to, anyway? In the year of revolution, a few guys occupied a tram line, showing disdain for the commuters who had to hurry to work on foot. But when they proudly related the blockade of public transport, they didn't prattle on about the injured and the dead, no, they didn't like to exaggerate. The truth was never sacrificed for the sake of a punchline, they could be relied on for that. And when could you ever not rely on them? They weren't risk takers, not even in love. Don't stick your neck out, as it was explicitly decreed on train windows in four languages. The local dialect didn't recognize anything as radical as 'I love you'. The most passionate expression, 'I ha di gärn'— 'I like you'—was the same phrase you would use for muesli.

'She's a dancer,' says the nurse with a sneer. 'Wait here for her.'

I recognize her by her gait: she totters towards me on high heels, her thighs pressed together. She's frank as she tells me her story, her voice smoochy through her pout. Every night until four in the morning she's a little plaything, purring for the men at the bar who are after a bit of Lolita at the end of the day.

'Do you have to sleep with them?'

'No, no. We just dance and strip. During the breaks we encourage the men to have a drink. I sometimes tip away the drinks they buy me. I can't take much alcohol.'

'Can't you refuse?'

'I'd lose my job.'

She shrugs. For the twenty-five-year-old these are simply the unpleasant corollaries of a major lottery win. She would rather strip in an affluent country than sit at a supermarket check-out back home for a pittance, getting harassed by the boss and ageing prematurely. She digs out the evidence of her good fortune, her tattered contract that says 'cabaret dancer'. She looks at me, waiting for encouragement. Then she hastily provides her justification. Her father died, and her mother was made redundant from the weapons factory. She stares, wide-eyed.

'Haven't you noticed, these are tough times, and I've got a four-year-old daughter.'

'Does your mother know what you're doing here?'

'Mama knows that I dance.'

She says the word 'dance' often and with emphasis, rehearsing her new identity. Dancing is an art, a recognized profession, for which she has to make her sacrifices.

'I can't put on a single kilo.'

She is merely a body, no longer a linguistically gifted being. What need has she of language when she carouses at the bar with the drunkards? Her shrunken vocabulary is limited to the word 'ciao' which she uses to greet everyone, including the doctor. Intimacy as a career dissolves the distinction between private and public. She hasn't finished her story yet. Here comes the happy ending.

'I've met a man, someone from here. He wants to marry me.'

Her words are ecstatic, a prospector who's struck gold. She stretches, then whispers, 'I can't decide. Should I leave everything behind?'

She expects someone who has also turned her back on her homeland to dismiss such rhetorical doubts: Why not? Go for it!

I don't say anything.

The gynaecologist leafs through the patient's file with a disapproving look on her face. 'If you're changing partners, you should always use a condom. The HIV and hepatitis C tests are negative. And the suspicion of a sexually transmitted disease hasn't been confirmed. It's only in the uterus that we've identified cell mutation.'

Something has changed in her feminine core.

'My stomach is swollen and is making noises. Am I pregnant again?'

The pregnancy test is also negative, the patient is overjoyed. The doctor's face tips from distaste to sorrow. The patient recently had a miscarriage above the clouds, when she was flying home for a holiday. A happy stroke of fate, as she wouldn't have an abortion. She does have moral principles, she insists. The talk of sheathed penises and spermicidal vagina cream is endless, my interpreting lacklustre. The young woman decides to have a coil fitted; she'll ask her impresario to pay for it.

As I convey her words, I make a slip of the tongue: 'repressario.'

I was too young for this grown-up, sensible country. My attempts to provoke it to fall madly in love with me all came to nothing. Like a young mother turning away from her ageing husband and lavishing all her passion on her son, I also placed my hopes on small children with that fluffy chick smell that transcends nationality. I wanted to inhale them, snuggle up with their soft bodies, melt into humanity. Children still belonged to the wilderness. With them I could be playful and carefree, stripped of the rigid, cultural corset. But of course, babies were also family property, you didn't trust them to a stranger's embrace. They were bestowed long names, as though they were dignitaries to be addressed formally. The parents spoke politely to them, keeping up the formalities, granting them an official kiss before they went to bed. If they treated their own babies like foreign diplomats, how were they going to act with me? They didn't tease their little ones, that would be a bit too much.

Prohibitions were reiterated solemnly and slowly: 'I've told you, no. You can't have that.'

I would then wait for the parents to rip up their words and break out into laughter: 'Only joking! Of course you can—here you are.' At which point they'd embrace their little bundles of joy, swing them in the air, and the joy would grow and grow and carry me away with it.

But no, they stuck to their word and never tore their rules up into pieces. They appealed emphatically to reason, preparing their children for the superficial world they knew so well. The possibility that beyond it lay a thousand other worlds and beneath it were a thousand layers, a thousand joys—that was a well-kept secret. It was a sham and I railed against it. When I broke their rules, they thought I was incapable of reason. They would start to enlighten me, but I would interrupt them. 'I know.'

They had offered me refuge in this best of all worlds and the thankless foreigner was ridiculing their philosophy of life.

In the sandpit, they admonished their offspring. 'That's not your bucket, give it back. Play with your own bucket. I bought it especially for you.'

If a child pressed his bucket against his chest, they praised him: 'He's learning to tell mine from yours. He's making wonderful progress!'

Back home, I had learnt to nip egotism in the bud, to share, to always be there for others, to share in others' worries, to consider others' misfortune as my own. But here, if I got involved in others' concerns, I'd be pushed away rather than praised.

'It's not your problem.'

'But everything that happens affects me somehow.'

Then I'd hear the extraordinary response: 'You just enjoy your own life.'

How offensive that sounded! No enjoyment could be more important than the heroic struggle for the common good. How miserly to devote myself to improving my own life. I didn't want to be so shrunk into myself, I had big plans. Anything that was a dirty word in our dictatorship, a punishable offence, was transformed here into an achievement of democracy.

'I'm an individualist, I'm not like everyone else,' the whole country would say as if with one voice.

I, too, was distinct from everyone else, but not in that way. I was a visitor from the moon. Back home everything was permeable, the doors in public toilets didn't lock, we were all one single, indivisible body. And I had been amputated from that body. A little finger drifting through outer space. If I expressed my anguish, people would suggest that I alone was to blame for not managing. I remained obstinate, refusing to be grateful for my forced marriage to the host country. I didn't recognize and didn't want any other happiness besides the fused-together and shared-out kind.

A classmate of mine earned her pocket money working Saturdays in a supermarket.

'But your parents are rich.'

She was amazed by my unwarranted confusion. 'Yes, they are, but I'm not. I have to learn to fend for myself.'

Everything had to be pedagogical; she had no need of wasteful charity. The poor child, I thought, with parents like that, but she was proud of her independence.

The family is all wrapped up in puffy, beige windbreakers to cushion them against the cold and any collisions. If you pierced them, all that would be left of the inflated protective shell would be a shrivelled plastic skin. But the threat of cold or impact doesn't come from the outside. The father's pallor sinks into deep, dark craters under his eyes. The mother's face, on the other hand, is steady, a barren expanse not disturbed by any facial expression. Her brittle hair droops like weathered grass from a rocky crevice. Her body has no elevations; she is flat in an emotional sense, too. A cool, chiselled figure. A girl and a boy play with a rope, tying each other up and rolling on the floor, before jumping up and running screaming through the offices of the family therapist. They imagine they're alone in a void, no matter where they are. A family of four, all of them pale, puerile and gangly, with the same mid-length blonde hair. A rope team without a leader. Their only wilful move was to seek out a new country.

My entire body tenses as if trying to snap the invisible ropes that have wrapped around me. The family mood seems to have carried over to me. The therapist also adopts a rigid posture and reports in a tragic voice that the kindergarten teacher needed to contact the authorities. Suspicion of physical abuse? Incest? No. The kindergarten teacher's only concern was their lack of punctuality. She sent a request for the parents to come and speak to her, but they didn't. We are sitting around a table in a country where people are judged according to their reliability with respect to time. Where this family comes from, time is weathered by the constant flow of all things. Interpersonal commitments come and go, swept up in the vortex of improvisation, vague thoughts of future plans simmer away to an overcooked mush.

The children are the same in their apartment, running around, grabbing a wooden block from the floor, a wheel, a piece of train track, then tossing them on the floor again.

Pieces could be combined to make constructions, but there are no instructions, no direction. Joy and curiosity have moved out and left a junkyard in their wake. The mother's only concern is her dark financial worries.

'Start a language course?'

'It's expensive.'

'Put the children in day care?'

'Who's supposed to pay for that?'

Depression, says the therapist, is a master of deception, it dresses fears up to look more respectable. Money worries— that sounds like a concrete reality. But it's just a bluff. The woman mutters that she's afraid her husband will lose his job. She's already lost him as a husband. He's dragged his mattress into the children's room, it's covered with Lego bricks, while she sleeps alone in their bedroom, with the blinds down. The children don't dare come in. As she walks absently through the apartment, we see the effect of her voracious anxiety. Her gnawed body must have swollen twice in the last few years, milk must have flowed from above her protruding ribs. We submit to the spirit of the household: no smiles, no flippancy. We aren't treated as guests, not even offered a glass of water. Anxiety is not a good hostess. She is lady of the house and she is on the prowl. I'm an interpreting automaton and the therapist is a vehicle for solving the riddle of life.

The children don't look at the visitors, they carry on with their manic, noisy laps. What looks like unrestrained energy is desperately undirected. Strangle marks are found on the girl's neck. The culprit? Neglect. The children were playing at *taking the dog for a walk, turning the mountaineering rope into a leash, while their mother was lying down in her room. She might also be found lying among the Lego bricks. The children would pick up their mother's lifeless body and toss it down somewhere else.*

Arriving late at kindergarten is a sign. The mother doesn't get up in the morning, doesn't send the children out into the world on time. She's on the ropes, floundering, holding the rest of them back. Now the husband is talking. He works as a programmer in another city. He travels back and forth every day, I interpret.

He corrects me. 'I commute. I'm a commuter.'

So, he knows the word. When he says that, he stands up. That is his identity, commuter between the worlds, he finds his equilibrium on the train, a pendulum between two cities, his loose community is on that commuter train. That's where his decision matured. Amidst the darkness of the bags under his eyes, there's a flicker of light.

'I quit.'

He's outdone himself, grown beyond his limits, beyond worrying about his family.

'I told my boss I was unhappy.'

The woman freezes as if she's been critically wounded. And then the man laughs, tense, baring his straight teeth at her fears.

The children suddenly stand still. They've pulled their hats down over their ears, buttoned up their padded windbreakers, their faces pressed up against the frosted glass of the front door. Ready to go.

I took refuge in nature; it would embrace me without reservation. En route to the summit, my companions looked for signboards to check what was forbidden. They didn't find any and were at a loss. Were we allowed to leave the hiking trails? Walk across a mown meadow? Bathe in the pond? Caprice lurked in such a landscape, they fumbled about gingerly. Their mood grew gloomy in the impassable undergrowth, just as I was perking up. Finally, a prohibition sign appeared—the holy grail! Standing tall and proud like a pert young woman, outlined in a beautiful red, the writing thick and black. My companions read its warning to me triumphantly.

From our dictatorship, I was no stranger to defying servitude—by treating the authorities as an enemy. The locals, eager vigilantes who were fond of slipping into the role of law enforcement, were keen to demonstrate that there was no authoritarian state here, only free citizens.

'If only an earthquake would come and bury their rules and schedules,' I whispered to Mara.

'Even earthquakes are predictable here,' she warned me.

And yet so many people here had a longing to send their God to Hell, just the once, at least. In the summer they drove to slovenly countries, where they became loud and lewd, unable to read the signs, spending more money than intended, returning home sheepish and shocked by their own behaviour, and went straight back to telling me off. At heart, they remained committed wardens of a home for those with learning difficulties.

A starving kitten found its way into our backyard. Who wouldn't feed it? The next day it was there again, meowing at me. After a few days, the neighbours confronted me. How dare I encourage a stray to get used to living here?

'You know what happens. First one puss, then hordes of the rascals.'

'But where do you see whole hordes?'

'One today, many tomorrow. If we tolerated exceptions, then where would we be? Cats either belong to someone or they're taken to an animal shelter.'

Instead, I continued bringing the homeless kitten food, and not even appropriate food at that. I wasn't exactly a cat expert officially entrusted with the task, capable of solving the situation long term in such a way that it wouldn't develop into a feline infestation. In our dictatorship, we were allowed to feed cats without a government permit. My neighbours put a sign up in the backyard: 'Feeding cats is prohibited.' I then started throwing food out the window, but was caught and denounced to the caretaker. A letter arrived by registered post; I was being threatened with legal action. Now I only sneaked food out at night. One morning I'd come out to find a bloody cat skin outside my door. But that was only in my head. They weren't that bloodthirsty here.

Oh, I got up to a speed hemmed in by all these fences! But the barriers didn't stop me, didn't slow me down, crashing into them became motion itself. Whereas the locals would pause, assuming they had reached their destination. 'We have it good here,' they said, a little ashamed that they had it so good, and keen for me to imitate their ways, so that I would have it good too, and then they wouldn't have to feel ashamed. It was fine for domesticated birds, but for this young bird of prey it was a cage. I was supposed to vacuum-pack all my experience, dispose of it as hazardous waste and start again from scratch. I looked pityingly at the locals as if their arrogance were an illness. Pity met with pity.

Then they shaved my head and packed me in sterile little boxes. No. I countered their obsessional neurosis with my hysteria and ran away screaming. To abandon my wild nature would mean to give up existing. I was raw flesh, and over it I wore my unruly fur. Just as long as I wasn't boiled and quartered, as was the custom here. I still knew nothing of metamorphoses and fought to keep my instincts whole.

First, I see an enormous belly, beside it arms dangling, only then numb eyes and a wide nose squashed by fate, through which the patient is breathing heavily. The psychiatrist's body offers an enjoyable contrast: an upper torso steeled by bodybuilding, squeezed into a tight-fitting sleeveless T-shirt, a thick head of black hair tamed into a ponytail at the back. When he says to the suicide, 'I am sad that you're unwell,' his professional grief seems in rude health.

The patient seems distant, replying with a one-minute delay like an overseas phone call. 'I'm falling, I'm falling.'

A dreadful weariness slows down the transport of words. He's come here from his war-torn country, now he doesn't want to go any further.

'If I kill myself, you won't notice, even if you're sitting by me.'

The psychiatrist pretends to be offended and touches the patient's arm. 'I'm not taking my eyes off you. I will take good care of you.'

'I'll pack my things on Friday, and you won't see me again.'

'The antidepressant takes a while to take effect. It won't kick in before Friday.'

'Friday isn't necessarily Friday,' I say, offering my inter-cultural insight. 'Friday could be Monday or Wednesday.'

In the patient's culture, time is negotiable.

But the psychiatrist looks at me suspiciously. I'm destroying fixed concepts like Friday is always Friday, you can take the patient's words at face value. It takes a while for the psychiatrist to trust this possibility that Friday isn't Friday.

He calls me on Monday. 'The patient is still here; we need you again.'

The patient sits there and yawns, without hiding the gaping void with his hand. He chews on his saliva.

'Are you still having suicidal thoughts?'

'What?' his wife interjects. 'This is the first I've heard of it. Wait, we need to talk.'

The wife is furious that he wanted to lie down under the ground and leave her with the children.

'Didn't you tell your wife?' the psychiatrist says reproachfully. 'She's worried.'

The suicide nods in shame. To kill yourself is immoral.

'He's been driving me crazy lately,' the wife complains. 'Doing laps of the apartment all day. I asked him, have you got a headache or a heartache? Soulache, he told me.'

The psychiatrist says to the patient, 'We are concerned about you.'

He is concerned that his department might find itself in difficulties if the patient kills himself shortly after being discharged.

'We'll up the dose of the antidepressant, to have more impact on the chemical processes in the brain.'

Two well-behaved toddlers look at their father with indifference and a little surprise, as if he were a broken toy.

Then the man braces himself to scream. 'Can you immunize me against depressive wars, dictatorships of marriage or the madness of emigration? Dose me up!'

He holds out his flabby arm to the doctor and rolls up his shirt sleeve.

There was a queue of people at the department-store check-out. Deep in concentration, focused on the goal, these queuers were not going to be distracted by anything. What would they even talk about in the absence of shortages? You couldn't even generate a little camaraderie and human warmth with a shared grumble. They made friends with the objects in their shopping basket. If I tossed a joke into the mix like a grenade, they wouldn't join in with a grateful laugh, they wouldn't arch their bellies forward or lean their heads back nonchalantly, they wouldn't drop their shoulders or let their eyes wander over the face of their roguish fellow citizen. No, they would lean in and fix me, disturber of the peace, with a charge of polite, silent anger. And I would never again touch their sacred tension that could produce enough current to light up a million or two households.

These people didn't stand for any nonsense, especially not when it came to money. No sooner was payment made, and concluded with a formal exchange, in hollow-sounding voices, jet-washed of any personal balderdash, than they set off for their next destination. No hanging around to risk losing composure. They looked as if they were deeply engrossed in interminable drudgery, to be freed only by death, that unknown idler. Their piercing gaze betrayed their focus on this earthly world; it was a gaze that focused on what stood to reason, unmasking even the minutest specks of dirt, always on duty, a detective for hire. Under their scrutinizing stare, I caught myself having mean, tainted thoughts. Their gaze never lingered in the clouds, unless, of course, they were tasked for professional purposes with searching the sky for suspicious specks. And of course, even then, it wouldn't be an indolent, cloud-gazing sort of gaze. But for all their vigilance, there were still occasions when they missed something, a failure never met with an indifferent shrug, but with renewed determination to banish the slightest speck of dirt with their double-sided brushes, special suction cleaning cloths and all the other paraphernalia for conquering the mundane that they lugged to the cash register.

Back home, you set your sights haphazardly, sceptical that you'd ever hit the mark. If you did, you celebrated, if you missed, well, you always could blame the dictatorship, the scoundrels at the top. Life was tough in a democracy. No need to celebrate after completing a task, straight on with the 'follow-up', a word that was impossible to translate. For every speck of dirt, someone was liable, someone was to be held accountable. They tormented themselves with remorse if a plan fell through, heroically proclaiming, 'I take responsibility.' I spelled out this mysterious word *Verantwortung* and found the *Antwort*, the answer, lurking within.

They were fighters, idealists of the material, relying on their tenacity, steadfast in their pursuit of the impossible: to keep the surface of their little world polished and buffed, and permanently, no matter what. No sooner was the bank counter scrubbed clean than the bacteria would amass, our most ancient ancestors creeping up on us. Again and again, the country went into battle with its primal ancestry, armed with their cloths and disinfectant spray. It was only in this country that I discovered that I had an innate visual impairment for dirt. After I had mopped the stairwell, the neighbours would call me back to inspect the invisible specks of dust. At least, we were having a conversation, finally. Not that there was any lack of self-awareness here. In darker moments, some grew weary of themselves, entertaining doubts about their best qualities. But the way you'd been brought up was ingrained; try as you might, you can't scrub it away.

'Why did you come here?' the psychiatrist asks.

'I was a slave, for ten months.'

The patient tells her story in short, clear sentences, for which I am grateful. Concentrating on linguistic communication helps me to keep the rising anxiety in check. I recognize severe trauma from the way the young woman wears her body as if it were a borrowed dress. At some point the soul said farewell to its female body, its spineless partner who had betrayed it. The body was sacrificed to save the soul. Now they've lost each other and can't find their way back. If the patient perceives anything of her body, it is only pain.

'My neck hurts.'

Looking straight ahead, as if she had blinkers on. A vital, narrow focus, saving energy. They don't like her in the refugee shelter. She screams at night but when they confront her about it, she has no memory of it. She quarrels with everyone, complains about children riding tricycles in the hallway. She shares the room with seven women of another faith murmuring unintelligible prayers, which she can't abide. She comes across as haughty. She can't take on anything new, she's full to the brim with her past. So many nations, loud voices. She demands a room of her own.

'I've lived through terrible things.'

To which comes the reply, 'Who hasn't?'

She hears voices calling her by name, turns around, but there's no one there. Recently she was walking in the street without even realizing that she was walking. She had walked out on herself. She wonders about it. Sometimes she sees a figure in the street that immediately dissolves, and an over-whelming force pushes her to the ground. The psychiatrist wants to find out whether the patient has also experienced self-determination. Her chances of treatment depend on it.

'Did you fight back?'

'What do you mean? I was always in the room. They would often beat me, on my legs, my kidneys.'

'Who were these men?'

'Bodyguards and politicians. I recognized some of the faces from television. Part of their income is from trafficking women.'

'Part of the training of the police and special units is a targeted blow to the kidney,' I explain to the doctor. But she isn't a detective who needs evidence like that to shed light on the case.

'I also saw the president there,' says the patient.

Does the psychiatrist recognize this as delirium? It may just be a harmless mix-up. Her president has a very ordinary face.

The patient speaks about men as though they were a dif-
ferent species. The more men abused her, the guiltier she felt.
The perpetrator doesn't feel any shame. She had her ID taken
away, to have one would render her human. When she asked
why, this was the explanation:

'You'll never need it again; we'll finish you off soon.'

The slave girl was to be sold abroad, three foreign buyers
ordered her to undress in a hotel, and when she was later left
alone with the bodyguard, she hit him on the head with a
chair. She ran for her life through the snow in her panties.

There was one man who respected her freedom. He organ-
ized and paid for the transport. She sat behind the cab of a
truck, protected by a second wall. A common method for
smuggling. The driver stopped now and then in the forest,
she'd have a wash and something to eat. After three days he
unloaded her.

'Now see for yourself how you get on.'

As a child, she had wanted to be a judge, to dispatch crimi-
nals off to prison. But she dropped out of school. Her mother
was a cook in the school canteen. Things were better after her
father moved out. Men were no good in their backwater. From
baby bottle to liquor bottle, and at the first sign of facial hair
they were drafted into the army. They then did time for theft
and brawling, and died before their time. Some boys acted
tough, puffed up their chests.

'Don't get involved with the mafia,' her mother had
warned.

At twenty-three she decided to move to the capital and promised to send her mother money.

'I have nightmares. My skin's peeled off, I'm dismembered. I've got this unbearable jumble of voices in my head that makes me want to jump out of the window.'

'Is there anything stopping you from jumping out of the window?'

'Thinking about Mama.'

The telephone connection with her mother is the only link to home. The psychiatrist goes out, comes back, arranges the objects on the table, then stands up again. She's shielding herself behind fussing.

'It's a difficult case,' she says to me. 'I'm going to refer her.'

Outside, I comfort the young woman. 'Try to live in the now and focus on those moments.'

'I go to the park, but I can't enjoy anything.'

'You're like a soldier who's come back from the front. You're still living the war, but you'll overcome it and help other women. Millions of women are slaves.'

'Me? Help? Now my neck hurts again.'

I've overwhelmed her. I want to hug her, but I'm wary of harassing someone who's so often had touch forced on her. And I want to get away from her. From her story. As a compromise, I gently squeeze her elbow.

Her hair went grey when she was imprisoned. She has dyed it jet black, thick make-up caked on her stone-cold face. Her ill-treated body is fashionably attired. She has internalized *the imposed cult of beauty. There are rumours in the refugee shelter that she was a woman 'of loose morals'.*

'Where on earth does she get her togs from?' one whispers.

The shame stains her like the dye from a damp, dark dress.

Months later she tells of a man who touched her for her benefit for once, with practised fingers, a physiotherapist, who manipulated the vertebrae in her neck. And the guard in the refugee shelter gave her a prayer book and said, 'Nothing happens without God.'

A novice now, she has a dream of redemption. She's in the dark in the middle of a crowd that is stamping her into the ground. She screams and, with all her effort, she pushes the crowd aside and stands up. She hears a child crying and bends over the small, bloody body. Suddenly it's lit by a beam, a great silence pushes the noise of people away and a voice resounds from the sky: 'All who have done evil will now die. Only the good will live.'

She sees people fall and the child rise up. She cries and prays in the blazing light until she wakes up.

If I left my hiding place, I would meet him. Everywhere I went, I was at his mercy. I would never be able to get a divorce. Like a frustrated wife letting off steam by complaining to her neighbours, I went round and round in circles with my litany of complaints about my husband, convinced this foreign land was preventing me from living my way. Whenever I got to know someone, I was handed a breviary to enlighten me on making acquaintances. If I tripped over, they would draw me up a map of the city marked with stumbling blocks and red exclamation marks. If I bought an apple, I'd be informed of the apple prices in the entire district. Newly enlightened, I would now certainly go out of my way to source the most cost-efficient fruit. Here, everything happened according to a system, whereas I was pure happenstance. To them, no one and no event was unique. They turned my improvisations into a regulatory framework, placing their faith in an eternal recurrence. Leading child psychiatrists recommended repeating back every repetition, but slowly, please! That worked better than valerian drops, they said. It all made me feel highly perturbed.

Obsessions were filtered according to topic. For a membership fee I would be welcomed into an association, club, group or advisory body. But where would I fit? Not yet at the developmental stage of specialization, I munched my way through everything, with a large spoon. A pre-industrial soul. I screamed outside the protected framework of a primal screaming group registered in the directory of associations. I wanted to talk to the roofer about being and not being, rather than about the roof tiles that needed replacing, I showed the washing-machine man all sorts of things, including the oven that was on the blink and the broken table leg, but he insisted on his exclusive honour as a plumber.

I was still living in a primordial drop of water, but there was already some cell division. Politically, too. The country prided itself on its separation of powers. But Mara was not impressed.

'Yeah, we know. Some exercise violence and others share it out.'

To help a girlfriend get a job was frowned upon as favouritism. The locals panicked at such improper interference. I was used to people helping one another. You had to if you wanted things to tick along like clockwork.

I elicited nothing from the shop assistants beyond business, they wore smiles like masks, their hands packed the goods tightly, careful not to leave a suggestive aperture peeping out to lure us mischievously from our purpose. If my dear fellow creatures wanted to show affection, they would hand me some artfully wrapped object. Accompanied by a well-crafted remark.

I had lost the right to give. If I gave someone something, I caused only embarrassment. It didn't make them happy. A gift from me plunged them into guilt and obligation. And into a connection with me. They felt obliged to reciprocate, to balance like with like. And what need did they have of my cheap trash? They possessed vast collections of valuable objects, atop the apex of the hierarchy of respect. This was a time-consuming cult they practised: gathering trinkets around the world, assigning them a permanent place in their stylish apartments, caressing them with their eyes. If any of their darlings were damaged, they were enraged, mourning their loss and calling in specialists who dealt with assorted cracks and rifts.

To turn your back on community and play the field with beautiful objects—this was a luxury afforded only to a society where elementary survival didn't depend on other people.

Back home, we invested everything in a dense web of relationships, we cultivated togetherness, empathized with each
other's whims, found consensus, and consolidated it with
touch. Best to try and please everyone, after all, you didn't
know who would be there to drag us out when it all went pear
shaped. A different matter when someone was out of earshot.
Then we let rip behind their backs. That built a connection.

In this country, brutal honesty was the order of the day.
No beating about the bush, they came straight out and flung
a brusque 'no' in your face. I wasn't used to this incivility, I'd
try to transform this 'no' into a subtle 'maybe' or an enthusi-
astic 'yes'. Scandalized, they wouldn't budge an inch. Loyal
to the end, they were always true to their 'no', but the same
fidelity applied to a 'yes'.

If I started to badmouth someone, they showed me the
shortest route. 'Go tell him yourself.'

I hesitated, ashamed. Let rip in open ground without
back-up?

They continued to nag me. If I dared postpone my visit to
the Botanical Gardens, they admonished me with, 'But next
time you stick to what we agreed.'

They ruled with a clear conscience, brandishing the sceptre
of a guilty conscience. When were we supposed to get to know
each other properly? They kept time on a short leash, for me
time was a swallow in flight, swooping in fast and steep. I had
barely taken flight before they were opening their diaries to
pin me down to an appointment. They wore their timekeeping
uniform everywhere, not just to the bank, this tight-fitting

jacket they never took off, even at the park. The clock was the archetype in whose image man was created. 'Look, here comes Twenty Past Eight,' they called, seeing the drooping corners of my mouth. They were always en route from one time marker to another, an eternity dissolving between them. If I refused to submit to this absolutism of time, a raging devil would burst out of the clock and scream, 'But it's five on the dot!' The dear people in turn offered me their assistance and took over the task of curating my future. If I did something to thwart the process, they'd get all tangled up like wires in some antiquated contraption, shouting, 'Wait a minute!' Improvisation was sand in the works of this unwieldy apparatus. Then the device was switched off and the deviation integrated into the programme. After the vexatious interlude, they warned me, 'No more schedule changes!' In that regard, they were unwaveringly consistent. Consistency. A word held in high regard.

I thought they were uptight, they thought I was erratic. If I looked absent-minded, they were seized with suspicion, as if I were maliciously dragging the whole country down into the morass. It was only on vacation that they began to envy my heinous interaction with time. They worked hard at it while they were abroad, yet still turned up for their camel ride bang on time. As for me, sigh, I was late again.

It isn't the war he's come from that torments him, it's this illness that prevents him from walking, from getting out of bed, that pushes his head forward. The thirty-year-old pushes one foot in front of the other, stops, sighs. He points to his hands, feet, elbows, back, pelvis and chest, and grimaces. This is the face, twisted in pain, that he has shown to all the countries he's crossed these past months.

I can't think of the word for 'joints', so I make do with 'bones'.

'Yes,' he nods eagerly, 'it's my bones. They don't let me sleep. What's wrong with them? Are they falling apart? Will I never have a family? Will I end up in a wheelchair? In the refugee home they asked me, are you an invalid?'

He's humiliated by the word, he sobs. Just as his body is slipping away from him, so too are his thoughts. He points to his head, turns it and lets it drop. He was in the psychiatric hospital for four days. They thought he was confused, but then he was released with the words, 'Your problem isn't in your head.'

The rheumatologist knows his craft. He gives guidance to his fears that are tearing in all directions.

'It's your psoriasis,' he explains. 'Ten percent of psoriatic patients also present with polyarthritis. The X-rays show inflamed joints. It's an autoimmune disease—the immune system is attacking your own body. We don't know why.'

So, it was war after all. Civil war on the territory of the body.

'What will happen to me now?'

'We will use medication to suppress the immune system. I assure you, your condition will get better, you'll be able to sleep. You'll be able to trust your body again.'

Finally, someone, a grey-haired fatherly man, is telling him that there's something in this chaotic world that he can trust. Wasn't it because of this mysterious illness that he set off on his journey, to find a wise doctor who might diagnose and cure his malady?

The doctor knows about the placebo effect of his words, he doesn't lie, he just leaves out the side effects of the treatment and speaks with the requisite firmness. The drug is very expensive. He names a sum for which, in the patient's home country, an assassin would be willing to kill dozens of people. So much money just for his own good. And the young man doesn't even need to bribe anyone. To have suffered is enough. Here, suffering has human dignity.

At first all he had was blotches on his back, then the chaos of war came to his country, and the psoriasis occupied his whole body. The patches got bigger and wandered from place to place like refugees carrying their belongings with them. Soon after, the psoriasis crept under the skin, explosions in the joints. Swelling in the knees, toes, fingers. His life was turned upside down.

'I've lost my family, I've looked for them everywhere—to no avail.'

His story of loneliness isn't without cracks. This is the version for the asylum procedure. The young man isn't an *adventurer but, rather, the pampered son of a large clan who have sent him out into the world so that he might recover and produce offspring. This is the grail he has to find. He is expected to return walking upright, with strong bones, not slumped in a wheelchair. He has to get to know his body, gather it together, bundle it up, including his thoughts.*

The wise doctor has given him directions. Today is the beginning of his return.

In this country people were happy cultivators of blame. Accusations were as common as compliments back home. A compliment isn't educational, it's mere corrupt flattery, stirring up a sugary atmosphere that clouds the mind. Compliments are wasted on undeserved, unverifiable, fleeting phenomena like beauty. I handed out compliments left, right and centre. I would praise someone's dimple, their dress or their hairstyle, and was considered obstreperous. To them, a well-aimed reproach spurred on perseverance, it was a whittling knife for the character. In this respect they were generous, lavish with their trivial wordplay.

'Mucky shoes, mucky conscience.'

'Hole in your mitt? It's draughty.'

A little hole opened up the possibility of acquaintance, though. A reproach was the royal road to another person. They sat behind their fortress walls, and to request admission with a trite kind word would raise suspicion. On the other hand, a good sturdy reproach created trust. For a long time, I didn't recognize their tactics of conquest and I felt unloved. Whereas in fact, encircled by criticism, I was the focus of their love. A tight-laced passer-by pointed out that my shoelaces were undone. As I hurried to do them up, a glint in his eyes showed he hoped to pick me up.

I made a bet with Mara. 'I'm going to have a huge affair with that splotch on my sweater.'

I shared my valuable insights with others. I saw a young foreigner cycling on a path through the park, the sun glinting on the leaves, when a passer-by blurted out, 'No cycling!'

I explained to the distraught cyclist, 'Don't worry. It's a chat-up line.'

She was out of breath, sweating. I left the lucky recipient of this amorous attention with a tissue and marched onwards through the country, always ready to help.

In our dictatorship we were free to flirt, to test out entry-level opportunities with random bus passengers, starting with complaining about the senselessness of existence and parting with meat shortages, or vice versa. And then, it was over, forgotten, and we were already on to our next adventure. Here, dalliances were a rare thing and had grave consequences. Carelessly cocking my head to the side could bring on a severe attack of marital anxiety, and one time I did in fact incur a marriage proposal. You had to admire the courage of that particular young man. Usually, elementary school provided the foundation for a stable marriage. Your classmate whom you've known from first grade wasn't likely to turn into her opposite, and if she did, well, there was a prestigious sleep clinic not far away.

When nobody spoke to me in the long corridors of the university, I reverted to my most slovenly gait—which I thought was particularly seductive—and stalked up to a couple of students. Horrified, they delved into the criminal code.

The alma mater took pity on me and sent her best sons to conquer me. A medical student kissed me cautiously on the riverbank.

'I don't feel anything,' I said.

'Has that always been the case?' he asked, concerned, like a doctor.

After my 'no' he didn't pull out all the stops but pulled out of the seduction project altogether.

A student of Economics planned the kiss in advance, outlining the appropriate conditions we needed to ensure and consulting me democratically in the process, but I left nothing to chance and stood him up.

A budding literary scholar invited me to the theatre, but I had to pay my own way. Afterwards, we went to a cafe and he generously treated me to a camomile tea.

'Wait until the waitress is gone,' he whispered. 'Then you can give me the money for the tea.'

Where were the heroes of love? Later a supermarket identified the gap in the market and organized flirting courses.

Mara dreamed of a red sports car and a man in a black leather jacket with whom she could speed along the autobahns. Once set in motion, we could no longer stay still, we were spinning on the inside, our restlessness brought to the fore. Many refugees bought a used car first, I bought a blue bike. When I was depressed, I pressed into the pedals, I flew past all the foreignness, it couldn't hurt me any more. I belonged to speed, I sped through red lights, veered onto pavements, hurtled the wrong way down one-way streets, tore down steep alleys hands-free, whizzed across squares and parks, ignoring the shouted curses of the pedestrians I passed. Every now and then I had to pay a fine, that was the rent for my mobile home, the first I could call my own.

'You have metastases in your lungs and spine. We will treat you, but we won't be able to cure you. Enjoy every week, every month,' the doctor explains calmly to the patient, as if this were something she said every day.

I interpret in a feigned benign voice and add, 'Enjoy every year.'

The patient takes it serenely. She lies here in the hospital, exhausted and satisfied, like a sprinter reaching the finish line. Her race began when she ran from village to village fleeing bombs and purges with her son in her arms. Her husband was dragged away at a checkpoint, taken off in an armoured car. She would have liked to wash his corpse, but it's probably in a mass grave by now.

'I want to live for my son, I brought him up well, he is obedient, he will do your country proud.'

'Our country isn't a paradise,' the doctor mumbles.

But the patient has her goal in mind. 'People respect human rights here.'

Amidst the noise of the bombers, the screams of the injured, and the silence of the dead, she heard about human rights. Human rights are an undamaged house with a large roof, where angelic beings in white lab coats tenderly inject you with chemotherapy.

'It won't be easy for you and your son,' the doctor warns. 'Being in a foreign country.'

'Foreign? The horror we left behind is what was foreign. No, we've come home.'

A cancerous ulcer has broken through the skin on her left breast, and she groans when she hasn't taken enough pain-killers. Her lower back hurts, too. This is where the cancer has spread from the breast. When she goes up stairs, the cancer in her lung makes it hard to breathe.

'Why did you let it get this far?' The doctor shakes her head.

Back when she was in the bombed-out hospital, she met women of all ages who sacrificed their breasts for the sake of a bit more life.

The gynaecologist felt a lump and issued the brusque decree, 'The breast must go!'

She had resisted, angry that she had already lost so much, and no one told her that her stubbornness would be fatal. If the bombs and torture don't get you cancer will, they say in her pacified country. Getting cancer isn't a violation of human rights. The international community won't impose sanctions.

Weeks later, the patient lies on her hospital bed, her back to the setting sun. The psychologist put on a broad smile that she no longer takes off. It's an essential part of her work gear.

The patient thinks it's real. She mumbles, 'Everyone is so nice.'

She is given morphine before the radiotherapy, it makes her dozy. She pins her hopes on submitting to it, as if the cancer were a despot and her acquiescence could appease him.

'I'll take the medicine, I'll be on time for the radiotherapy. Others wouldn't take it seriously and would show up late.'

The psychologist is well versed at sowing doubts. 'What if the medicine doesn't work?'

'God decides, not the medicine. God will let me live.'

'And what if God decides otherwise?'

The psychologist takes her hand with a practised grip. 'Have you told your son how things are?'

The patient looks at me with venom, as though this drilling came from me. She addresses me by my first name, hissing like a snake rising to defend itself. I can hardly stand her gaze, which sometimes attacks, sometimes begs for good news. Suddenly I stop caring. I don't have to bring the whole person across on the language ferry, just her words.

The psychologist is keen to close the case. 'I'm sure you've prepared your son well for life. Do you have any relatives in your country?'

'No, my husband is dead.'

I've heard from her compatriots that her husband lives with a younger woman and has five children with her. The son has a father he could be sent back to after her death. However, if he is registered as fatherless, he could stay here as an unaccompanied minor. A stale aftertaste lingers on my tongue that has to find the language to clothe this lie. The head of the interpreting service gave clear instructions on the subject of 'lies': 'It is not the interpreter's job to seek the truth.'

The psychologist bids me farewell. 'We won't need you again. The tumour is spreading quickly. The patient could fall into a coma at any time.'

But she lived another year and a half, and shortly before her death she returned to her country to die there. Her son went with her and has lived with his father ever since.

Mara and I were searching for routes into the locals' hearts. You were fine as long as you could figure out the way.

'Bisch zwäg?' was how you showed concern for someone's well-being. 'You well?'

I proceeded on to fieldwork and asked walkers for directions, who went out of their way to help and even led me personally to my destination. As we walked, they spoke tenderly about forks in the paths. Then I started experimenting on dogs. I said hello to a bulldog that jumped out at me, asked its name and was showered with a wealth of information about its diet and stool consistency. The dog owners were refreshingly talkative, but they stayed on topic and didn't make the leap from animal to human needs. If I wanted to change the subject, I would have to make an appointment. Back home, if I paused at a fork in the road to chat to a passer-by about his pug, I would only need to read the clues to see if he was trying to pick me up.

Mara found that back pain was an even better way of scoring some affection. Never had we found the country to be more willing to assist than when arched forwards in pain. Perhaps the free citizens thought we were bowing to them and were touched by our reverence. They asked sensitively whether they could help us onto the bus. Having mutated into our personal nursing staff, they wanted to know where we lived, since when and on which floor. To them such questions represented the boldest kind of intimacy. After that, they were plagued by guilt that they had overstepped the mark.

The hospital was heaven within four walls. The patients received regular doses of recuperative attention, including touch, this rare commodity that not even parents squandered on their children. In their training courses, nurses and thera-pists were taught that physical contact was part of the job—unfortunately, yes, but that was the way it had to be. They were so diligent in their physical contact that it felt almost natural, it was delivered in conjunction with a word of comfort lifted from the textbook and an empathetic nod. The terminally ill had it best. They were also granted a pat on the head. Hidden behind the hospital walls was another country, a realm where lax morals prevailed, where criticism was banished, where abundant praise was lavished for an obediently swallowed spoon of Mehlsuppe. The hospital was a land of milk and honey. I once spent three days there, and afterwards I experienced withdrawal symptoms whenever I passed by.

Praise was also possible outside of clinical settings. If Mara said, 'I speak Germany but little,' she received uproarious accolades. People spoke loudly to foreigners, their impairment believed to be linked to their hearing. They were disabled, at any rate, and you were kind to disabled people. Education for disabled people was highly developed. They weren't hidden away in dark rooms, but led out in groups, walking arm in arm with their one-to-one supervisors. Unfamiliar weaknesses were seen as endearing, lovable. However, if the weak should presume to gain strength beyond a tolerable level, that love was soon withdrawn.

Mara and I imagined a threatening scenario: a large group of beautiful people arrive in the city and their radiating beauty triggers a nuclear siren. Only the stove was supposed to sparkle, not the housewife. When my neighbour was awaiting her lover, she scrubbed the sink instead of herself. She knew where the loving male gaze tended to fall. The kitchen was an extension of the female body, after all. 'Greetings to the kitchen' was what men said when they wanted to send kind regards to a friend's wife.

'This country needs pets, disabled people, and foreigners,' said Mara.

At the sight of vulnerability, people shed their timorous paralysis. The inhibition threshold dropped, the locals could abandon their formal manner and speak as freely as they had been trained. Very convenient. It was with relish that they could chasten both their frolicking dachshunds and any precariously tottering foreigners they happened to encounter. They evolved into zoo directors, kindergarten teachers, special-needs consultants, family therapists and integration officers, all in one. And bank clerks. In the distant realm of money—and this I knew only from hearsay—the penny-pinching perimeters stretched far and wide. There was demand for growth, for the multiplication of euphoria. Valuable feelings were stored in safes, insured against thieves on the outside, but not against the masked ones on the inside.

Oh, the poor heart! Suppressed by an overbearing colonial ruler. As soon as we realized how the country covertly longed for independence, longed to drag their intimidated hearts out into the fresh air, we were off. It was easy for Mara and me to cry, to swear eternal friendship, to snuggle up to tense bodies, to betray our intimate thoughts—and then walk away as though nothing had happened. For us, the moment that counted was when the flames burned high. But what remained was just scorched earth. Our irrepressible manner met with fear and distrust, not to mention envy. Some took our exuberance as the beginning of a lifelong friendship, they gingerly pushed open the back door to let us in, but we didn't even notice, we'd already erupted elsewhere, ephemeral, panting. We soon had a reputation for being a danger to the public.

But we were just on the wrong track, sprinters who had accidentally found themselves in a marathon.

A tall young man is waiting at the refugee advice centre. He doesn't look traumatized. Nor does he look shifty. Pretty well kempt, in fact. He has never had any ID, he doesn't even know what such a thing is.

'Without proof of your identity, you could have difficulties with the authorities,' says the social worker. 'Can your parents get you some ID?'

'My parents died in a house fire when I was little.'

'How did you go to school without any papers?'

'I didn't go to school.'

'So can you read or write?'

'Yes, my grandmother, whom I lived with in the village, she taught me.'

Then he also declares the grandmother as dead—without the slightest wavering in his voice. On the third day after her death, he went alone to the capital. The young man doesn't seem to be aware that after someone dies there's a funeral, and for the only descendant, there's winding up the household, and the inheritance proceedings.

The social worker has a heavy accent, she was a refugee herself. She advises the adolescent to tell the truth when speaking to the refugee agency officials, not to get tangled in contradictions, and to answer all their questions. His fate depends on the hearing, which will last several hours. He'll have to grin and bear it.

'I went to a demonstration in the capital and was arrested. The police beat me and forced me to sign a statement saying I had committed some robberies. They needed a perpetrator for their unsolved cases.'

He also says all this effortlessly. Apparently, it wasn't until he reached the refugee shelter that he experienced any prison-like constraints. He was denied dinner because he was five minutes late and he was locked out one night—he had to spend the night in the park. He's beside himself at all this injustice.

'Those are the refugee agency's rules. You have to stick to them.'

To cheer him up, she congratulates him on not being housed in a nuclear bunker several metres underground, where he would have to share a room with nineteen refugees from various countries.

'I couldn't stand that,' he murmurs, startled, and complains that the guards call him a mafioso.

'Ignore them. They've had bad experiences with your compatriots.'

He says he met someone from his country who was an addict and who tried to entice him into some dodgy dealings, but an older refugee warned him, 'Be wary, look people in the eye. If their eyes are hazy, keep your distance.' Then he said to the drug addict, 'You have your way, I have mine.'

'You did well.'

His voice becomes mechanical again, his narrative style sober. He claims to have smashed the window in the judge's office when he left the room. He jumped out of the window.

'That still isn't a reason for asylum. Can you prove it?'

'No.'

'Do you have any health issues?'

'No, I'm well.'

'That's good, at least,' says the social worker. She never smiles, not even when she shakes his hand.

Outside, she hastily lights a cigarette and speaks to me wearily.

'After the hearing he'll be sent to the deportation centre for weeks, even months, until his country accepts him back. If he were genuinely a minor, as he claims, it would be more difficult, but his wrist measurements were taken on arrival. They always mix a little politics into their stories to sound like they've been persecuted politically. The smugglers recommend it. Sometimes I feel sorry for these guys.'

She inhales deeply. Her influence is extremely limited. Her face shows resignation. And yet she rebels by breaching confidentiality like this. Did she allow herself to because we're both foreigners? We look at the prison, which is next to the refugee home. A hand waves to us through the bars.

The locals had a kind side, which I noticed when I caught myself being unkind. Foreigners were given the privilege of being allowed to rattle on non-stop, as though someone whose life had been shaken by fate couldn't bear interruption. I let myself be seduced and betrayed my untidy thoughts in lengthy monologues. They listened with a melancholy nod, giving away nothing about themselves—that would earn the diagnosis of 'disinhibition'—but encouraged me to document discrimination so that they could be outraged at the cruelty of their fellow countrymen. These compatriots of theirs wanted to halve the number of foreigners and argued mathematically that half as many foreigners would pose only half as much of a threat to their own people. The country was split down the middle. Those who were drawn to foreigners rushed to shield them but also use them as a human shield in this civil war of ideas. They fought with a venerable solemnity corresponding to the gravity of the situation. They knew how difficult it could be here. They asked, full of concern, 'Are you eating healthily?'

I was care-free and worry-proof, although caring and worrying were valuable commodities. No sooner did you reach adulthood, than you had to start agonizing about retirement. But no need for apprehension, when you pay into your pension. There were carers to care for those who needed care, and when that came to an end there was aftercare. It was caring that had brought the country to maturity, from care to welfare. There was tireless promotion of caring that made life so carefree. But in fact, caring was just a fancy word for perfectly ordinary fears. A look through the caring spectacles demonstrated a pragmatic sense of civic goodwill. Idle care-lessness was looked down on by the condescendingly caring elite.

That I slept so deeply was suspicious; insomnia was the responsible route to a good night's curfew. Sleep was out of the question when everyday life brought with it a gruelling schedule of questions to be resolved by democratic means. Who would be appointed as the new officer for taking out the rubbish? Could the cellar key have a red ribbon? Was it not too political? A meeting was called, an agenda drawn up, the problem investigated from every conceivable angle, with everyone invited to fully express their views. It was a civic duty to form an opinion on everything under the sun. The structure of a model discussion was taught in schools for social workers and from there it spread like an epidemic throughout the population.

The assembled attendees valiantly endured their demo-cratic burden. They listened to each other and contradicted one another, albeit objectively, with deference to the rules of decorum. The focus was on what was small, feasible, immi-nent. To discuss anything beyond the foreseeable, plannable and actionable was as pointless as trying to build something out of smoke. What can you make from smoke? Well, smoke rings. One detail after another, one meeting after another, dawdling along, and again and again the same open question: 'Does everyone agree?' Whereas anyone damaged by dictator-ship had the urge to take action, make decisions, take off the brakes and get on with it. If I yawned, I revealed that I was in need of improving, and the democratically socialized attendees paraded their sadistic side, yet again hammering in the most tedious points until there was space in my head for enlightenment to seep in. Could I sneak away, never to be seen again? Not a chance, the programme was already circulated for the next meeting. The tedium had to be endured heroically without a murmur, a feat that was celebrated as a political achievement. They were convinced that the poor people who had been downtrodden slaves to a dictatorship had never known what a blessing it was to be bored.

Finally, after the laboriously achieved consensus, a new statute was drawn up, the haze of ideas was contained, and someone was assigned responsibility in a free and fair ballot. But the birth of new regulations was unaccompanied by the screams of labour. Even with the impending arrival of small citizens, the locals didn't shout and scream in childbirth like foreigners did. You don't scream in an office, and the whole country was an official space. Parents gave their toddlers their *Ämtli*, their officially designated chores, like parents elsewhere in the world doled out sweets.

'You collect the crumbs from the table, you wipe away the sweat, you crack the nut.'

The day was full of endless tasks and crumbs, the sweat dripping on the little nut.

'No pocket money until you've done your Ämtli. We'll let you off this once, but not next time.'

Childhood was functionalized, regulated like a road-safety training park. On Sundays, the little ones were taken to these places to storm about amidst the practice traffic lights. They were taught to recognize stop signals from a distance. The mind learned early on when and where to stop: at every juncture, lest ideas raced about and crashed into each other.

'What is the point of it all?' I asked like a depressed megalomaniac.

'Watch out! It's red,' came a voice bringing me back to earth.

While elsewhere young people looked up to revolutionaries dying a bloody death, here it was prudent driving instructors who were the role model for the young. Revolutions were viewed from afar, with a shudder and with a reassuring reminder that, here, we've long since overcome such backward violence. There were no warning signs reminding them of their own backwardness: 'Caution, derelict status of women! Danger of collapse! We assume liability.'

'If you were put on a plane home tomorrow, what would you do?' the psychiatrist asks.

'No one would manage it. I'd rather die.'

'Why did you flee to our country of all places?'

'Doesn't the whole world say that this is a humane country? Everyone trusts this country with their money and their secrets. I thought I was in good hands here.'

'You bet everything on one card and lost.'

The patient begins to shake violently, first her hands and chest, then her legs. It's over thirty degrees, but she's wearing a black woollen sweater, as if that could help with her lack of a home.

'Our job is to protect your mental and physical health, but within the framework of the law. We can't intervene in the negative asylum decision made by the migration authority.'

The psychiatrist repeats each thought three times, not even bothering with a different choice of words. I interrupt him, interpret briefly and succinctly. He's astonished, this tall, angular man, used to an audience that doesn't contradict.

People reveal themselves in their first few utterances. Interpreting is fire and brimstone, everything burns, all that remains is gold. Once I interpreted for a social worker who got so worked up at every petty little thing that her throat burned red. She repeated everything, and emphatically, and she complained to the head of the interpreting service that my translations were much shorter than what she had said. I'm a recycler who only rescues the most serviceable items from the garbage.

The psychiatrist works with insincere solemnity, feigned sympathy and standardized questions. He doesn't allow himself a single spontaneous hand movement. An uninspired performance bereft of linguistic or expressive richness. They learn psychology like driving a car. If you come to a dead end, you go into reverse. It's only when his phone rings and a child's voice calls out 'Papa' that the psychiatrist becomes a human being, who laughs and whispers, 'Hello, darling.' Then he goes back to being the empty, flat surface the patient can project everything onto.

Apparently, the ploy works because she says, 'I feel like you understand me.' Then she urges him, 'Make me better.'

I sit next to her and feel ashamed for my fellow woman. Opposite us is a wall of four men—beside the lead psychiatrist are three young registrars, studiously making notes, forcing their way into her, to take her apart. Later, they'll talk shop amongst themselves.

When the patient confesses that she was too cowardly to kill herself, the psychiatrist hopes she'll preserve this virtue.

'Can you give me your word that you won't harm yourself in our clinic?'

They solemnly shake hands across the table. This is a ritual act when dealing with attempted suicides. The patient is invited to make a pact with life. They're raised to the rank of a worthy contractual partner, they're held accountable. Suicide would be a breach of contract.

The psychiatrist says something more powerful than any contract. 'I'll write to the migration authorities and tell them you're in an acute phase of self-harm. It will take a few weeks for the drugs to work before you're stable. You won't be fit to travel in that period.'

The patient thanks him profusely, and the psychiatrist gives her an unrevolutionary nugget of wisdom as food for thought, which he considers realistic and therefore healthy: 'You're looking for justice, but there is no such thing in life. You know what happened to the prophet who walked the path of righteousness.'

In a park, the law of the jungle doesn't apply, the survival of the fittest with its gestures of intimidation. Puffing yourself up, raising your voice, devising underhand tactics to achieve your goal—none of that worked here. It was enough to carry out your task conscientiously. You weren't faced with a hundred obstacles a day that you had to overcome in endlessly innovative ways. My instincts were slackening, and the people seemed so insipid—yet more proof of how pleasantly civilized everything was here. You hardly ever had a blown fuse, except in body and soul. The only reason you might burn out was all the safeguards.

Also popular was demonstrative uncertainty. People loved to hedge their bets by tagging their words with a questioning '. . . yes?' This was to preclude the impression of unseemly confidence in their own wisdom or of wanting to inhibit democratic discussion. Ending every utterance with '. . . isn't it?' or '. . . right?' encouraged a friendly atmosphere, positioning yourself as a polite person who was capable of admirable self-doubt. Best to avoid arrogant self-confidence, right? Of course, they were in fact unshakably convinced of their own mind; the important thing was to maintain appearances.

Keen to show how well integrated she was, Mara started modifying her greetings accordingly. 'Grüezi, right?'

This country's pride and joy was its modesty. When the wealthy strolled out of their mansions, they wore baggy grey sweaters with faded jeans. If anyone stood out in the crowd for ostentation and colour, it could only be a tasteless refugee. The Minister for Economic Affairs took the tram, the Minister for Education travelled second class on the train. They both paid their way, possibly not with taxpayers' money. My favourite was the thrifty Finance Minister, who cycled everywhere and wasn't even flanked by a column of armoured cars. If I overtook him, he gave me a friendly wave. The Minister for Home Affairs even walked, feeling the land with his own two feet. The only ones on their high horses were prissy little girls trotting out laps around worn-down tracks.

In their front-garden idylls, they bid visitors farewell with, 'Take care of yourself!', their eyes overshadowed by looming dangers. Children were used to seeing Little Miss Careful as their first caregiver, followed by all their fearful relatives. And yet people died. Unspectacular deaths, obviously, but nonetheless.

'They should put the newborn straight into a coffin and keep the lid open a crack until it's time to slam it shut,' said Mara.

The context for this was her belly, which was beginning to bulge. The strategic approach here was to think, 'Where I am I may as well stay. Why swap a nice warm spot for one in a draught?' If the foetus had got itself cosily ensconced in the mother's womb, there was no reason for it to be banished, so abortions were forbidden. A violation of one's own belly was punishable by law. The work that had begun should be completed, never mind that in the meantime Mara no longer felt inclined. A foetus was also a contractual partner, after all. Back home, contracts were broken willy-nilly, and many a foetus fell by the wayside. When Mara asked the gynaecologist for an urgent breach of contract, her reply was clear: 'Have the baby and give it up for adoption.'

Fortunately, there were other countries beyond the border where work could come to an early completion. Mara returned with a belly sucked empty.

'Why do you think your son isn't speaking yet?' asks the child psychiatrist.

'Because he's shy,' explains the father. When he opens the kitchen door in the morning, he approaches the breakfast table with hesitant steps without looking at his parents. He's very wary of anyone he doesn't know. He's three but can still say only three words: Mama, Papa and no.

The mother nods, smiles with her eyes lowered, and now and then she whispers something to the husband. He rubs his big, rough hands; he's embarrassed about the whole thing. But it has to be done. Their son's mutism is a serious matter. They've come here with the thought of a mighty shyness that stifles speech, and over the long months it's become established within them as their magical formula. The family of four are clearly anxious not to stand out, as though there were a gene for shyness. Their clothes are light brown, they have a slinking gait, their faces are expressionless, as if they're intent on hiding themselves away. The parents' terse speech is limited to quiet exhortations to the children not to walk off, not to touch anything. They don't associate with people from their own country, there's too much resentment and discord in the small community.

'Can your son get dressed and tie his shoes?'

'We don't know, we get him dressed.'

The doctor turns to the boy. 'Where are your knees? Where's your elbow?'

The parents are astonished at the thought that we even have body parts and might need words for them. They're ashamed. But the boy can do something: he can catch a ball and throw it back with some force. A moment of joy and strength sweeps through his small body. Yes, he has a body.

The two-year-old daughter observes the unusual goings-on. She sits next to her father, pale and rigid. She too only says the same three words as her brother.

'My daughter will speak,' says the father, as though words were a hail shower you could forecast. He immediately falls back into his immense existential shame.

'The son sits at the computer all day, and she copies him.'

'That is harmful,' says the doctor.

War is harmful, disobedience is harmful. The father flexes his untrained thinking muscles. No authority has ever declared that computer games could harm young children's speech and were therefore to be prohibited.

'If we don't let them play, they cry,' he justifies himself.

The virtual realm has swallowed up the body together with the unborn language. Body and language. A pair of lovers, murdered on a daily basis.

In the street I take the boy's hand, stomp my feet and start running. The father calls to him not to tire himself out. But the boy runs with me, trips over and gets up without complaining. He tears himself away from the past, he isn't anxious with this person who's leading him into an animated future. Again, he stumbles and falls. A word falls out of his mouth, like a piece of apple stuck in Snow White's throat, a real word of three syllables. A word that gives birth to a world. One day the speaking boy will come back to the past from his distant future and bring his parents words like hard-earned banknotes, for them to build a house with.

A premature happy ending. At the next appointment, the doctor shares his diagnosis.

'There's a congenital defect in the part of the boy's brain that processes sounds and converts them into speech.'

Early intervention can help to build a modest house of language.

Suddenly they laughed. I was startled. They were laughing heartily at bright, simple jokes that were as innocent as daisies. Everything cost something, but the laughter that we had had to work hard for under the dictatorship was free here. As they loosened up, my facial muscles tensed, trained only to relax in the dark abyss. They were criminally negligent when it came to jokes, they didn't hone them into shape, structure them into any format, or furnish them with an ingenious punchline. To them, a joke was supposed to be accessible to all classes, transparently honest, never ambiguous—that would just be mean. Everything at the right moment. Serious food in the cooking pot, light-hearted fodder in the bird's crop. To smuggle a joke, heaven forbid a perfidious one, into a serious, respectable sphere would be an attack on democracy. Jokes were a leisure activity and were not supposed to be arduous. Why would you toil away for the sake of a joke? Did you get any money for it? In any case, only men were allowed to be funny. Women were responsible for the comfort of the home, and that was where the fun stopped. They had a reputation for being practically minded. The roast might burn if they were to start serving up witticisms. Once the house was tidy and the husband well fed, he would come over a little philosophical, rustling up an anecdote to accompany dessert.

Then there were the autonomous individuals who refused to rely on other people's jokes. They guffawed at their own remarks, regardless of whether they contained a germ of hilarity. The sad compulsion to laugh only disappeared when I spoke of atrocities. One popular comedian did nothing but talk and act the way people normally did. He didn't exaggerate anything, was lovably naive from the get-go, no danger at all to the public, and in the evenings they chuckled in front of the television at their own harmlessness. But their very own comedian, who always paid tax on his performances, yes, he was allowed to mock them.

Every year, they erected a stage on the riverbank. Local comedians came up with old jokes and won prizes for them.

'Where are the women in this country?' I asked, indignant.

'You're one,' said Mara.

I climbed up onto the podium, frantically recited a revolutionary poem, and the river valley echoed with a language never heard here before. The audience forgot to laugh, it was quiet before the applause came. I was given second prize. This was how I managed to get public recognition—as a comedy act. The time was ripe for foreigners to step up as entertainers. Idiosyncrasies were suddenly welcome, the rules could be broken—but, please, only on stage. No longer just wielders of jackhammers, cleaners and geriatric carers, this revolutionary appearance on the riverbank stage heralded the new era of the immigrant clown.

The foreigners circled around the frosty edges, easily disconnected, hovering a while on the outskirts, before heading off to other fringes and abandoning those too. They couldn't break into the protected inner circle, and who would want to at the price they were asking? True, there were a few risk takers. They sought out customs from local folklore, declared them under threat of extinction and became their ardent defenders. The hymn would unite the country, it had to be sung before every public event and at kindergarten every morning before they could play blind man's buff. They urged the locals to cling to their obstinate ways. At meetings, they insisted, 'We appreciate your democracy better than you do, because we know dictatorship. Don't squander this great asset. Chuck the bad foreigners out of the country, just keep us, the good ones.' They tried out the local dialect and wore the local garb. They didn't avoid the role of the clown, they fell headlong into it.

In the waiting room of the department of internal medicine, a woman sits with her heart on her sleeve. These are fleshy affairs of the heart. Every month she slaughters a sow in her village, freezes it, and travels day and night to bring it here. Then she consumes the sow with her new husband. She won't inherit his house or land, they'll go to his children and grand-children, but she'll get something out of it, she confides in me. No, she doesn't need to be able to talk to the old man, she just looks after him and does the housework. She doesn't have anything else to say about life in this foreign country. The family she's left behind, on the other hand, provides plenty of juicy gossip. Her language is like that sow, streaked with fat.

Her son, the good-for-nothing, discovered his unemployed father, the bastard, in bed with some woman or other in the middle of the day, then the father got pissed out of his mind and beat up the daughter, the slut, who got herself pregnant by some crook with a criminal record, the prick, so then she needed a shotgun wedding. All this costs money, which of course Mama helps with, the silly ass. Mama is only welcome home when she shits golden coins. She's always loaded when she gets on the bus.

'That's how it is,' she sighs.

But she isn't stupid, she says, she salts her gifts with a tirade of ranting. Her ex is afraid of her, she can really get violent, she boasts. The pastor needs to be properly remunerated, the baptism is coming up. She's also got political views.

'The politicians, those assholes, they've ruined our country.'

She used to toil away as a baker's assistant in her village, she had to get up before dawn. She developed a flour allergy and used to sneeze on the wretched baked goods.

A friend's advice turned the tide. 'Go abroad and be a geriatric carer like me.'

So, no more sex for her in this foreign country. When she told her friend she no longer remembered what the male apparatus even looked like, she was invited over for an inspection.

'Come to the nursing home, you can see one here, no problem.'

The head of the interpreting service has issued guidelines on proximity. Closeness is incompatible with our job, neutrality is at stake. We're not allowed to get to know the clients or talk to them in the waiting room. I don't stick to that rule, but since the warning, one of my colleagues always sits with a hard stare, avoiding eye contact to stop her compatriots from asking her how many children she has. She suffers from it, feels like a traitor. I advised her to bounce the question about children back to any curious parties. Most of them wouldn't notice if you didn't answer, they only counted their own children anyway.

It's early in the morning, there's a waft of alcohol fumes in the sterile hospital air, a flutter of hands. The patient's rosy cheeks announce the dawn.

'Morbus,' murmurs the doctor. She asks the patient about her daily alcohol consumption.

'Oh, only when guests come, a vodka orange, a glass of red wine, watered down, two or three Schnapps, not a gram more.'

'But your liver is in a bad way. The blood level shows your alcohol consumption must be extremely high.'

The patient starts to sound irritated, as if she were talking to her bastard family. 'Don't you drink anything when you have guests?'

She turns to me, hoping that I know how to respect the iron laws of sociability.

'Have you had another fall?' asks the doctor.

Yes, fate—evil, impervious fate—keeps mowing her down. Once, just like that, out of the blue, on the street outside a restaurant. She was in the emergency room before she came round.

'And recently I was standing in the kitchen with a steaming hot pot of soup, and wham, I was on the floor—with a scalded cunt.'

Ashamed for my compatriot, I interpret that as 'with scalded private parts'.

The essence of the interpreting profession lies in the eradication of one's own personality. If your interlocutors no longer notice that someone is interpreting them, you've achieved perfection. If I manage to disappear in this way, I wait it out on the speech conveyor belt, then resurface in full size after my shift and reveal myself as someone gifted with reason and emotion.

I admonish the doctor for being too indulgent with the patient, for encouraging him to see himself as a victim. I trespass into the psychiatrist's territory:

'Have you noticed that the patient has a sense of humour? You could make use of this source of strength.'

No, the psychiatrist, devoid of any humour, does not wish to comment.

My rebellion isn't over yet. 'In this country people only like foreigners when they're sick in hospital, woe betide them if they become too self-assured.'

The language horse has thrown off its rider. He's stammering, in free fall, trying to pull me back on the right path. He suggests Thursday afternoon for the next appointment, but I'm already off, galloping cross-country, mane billowing in the wind. Then the guilt kicks in. But I'm unable to submit to authority.

The head of the interpreting service warned me, 'We shouldn't do this job too often. It can make you ill.'

If the locals complained they were skint, I'd offer them some loose change. But they insisted it was just a cash-flow problem and didn't want to dip into their savings. To be strapped for cash was like being stripped bare, it was indecent, and borrowing money was an abuse of friendship. Their best friend was the Cantonal Bank. Thanks to banking secrecy, wives didn't know how much their household's breadwinner earned.

The cantonal government issued recommendations for all households on how much pocket money a ten-year-old should get and how little housekeeping money a housewife should get. After supper together at 6 p.m., the ten-year-olds and wives gave their accounts of their day's expenses. If the head of household was understanding about profligacy, the wife might be allowed a free hand with the supermarket tokens.

They believed not only in being able to direct their own destiny, they also forged favourable conditions for it. A youth savings account paved the way for the newborn to enter society. Saving over generations had paid off. The descendants didn't have to scramble about for every plate of liver and roast potatoes, they could spend their free time lounging in leather armchairs, leafing through foreign philosophies, undertaking educational trips, and indulging in cultivated delights.

Expensive restaurants were a safe space for thrilling experimentation. You obtained a trustworthy tip-off, reserved your table in good time, and full of suspense, you moved the food back and forth in your mouth. Only now did the whole range of human emotions unfurl, superlatives pouring out over the sauce, and as they chewed, memories of family meals and business lunches paraded before their eyes, as they compared quality and prices, side dishes and wine, service and the ambience. This was a realm beyond the usual rules. Here, over the starched white tablecloth, it was perfectly acceptable to lose your rag if, say, the wine was insufficiently chilled. These customers brimmed over with self-confidence. They knew exactly what to expect for their money and tipped the staff according to their subservience. The free citizens were entitled to a large selection of elaborate dishes. 'Try this, try that, what do you think?' I was initiated to the sumptuous game of democracy, but I was democratically unsuitable and had just potatoes without the olives and tap water.

Then I got a job as a waitress, clumsily serving tables with a gloomy expression. One evening a young businessman slipped me a large banknote.

'I don't deserve that,' I said. 'I'm hopeless at this.'

'That's why. I'm fed up with the usual stiff manner.'

I didn't stop to ponder whether he had offended me, but pocketed the undeserved reward.

This was the start of a steep decline in service.

If you heard someone boasting, it could only be a foreigner, and the country encouraged them down from their pedestal with a conciliatory wave of both hands. 'Come on, down you come.' No need for a fly over, keep your feet on the ground. To downplay oneself was respectable, showing off was suspect. A braggart can't be trusted, not even with selling stamps. Anyone who was too sure of themselves tended to live alone here. Lonely and bereft of postage stamps. A show-off was a pernicious egomaniac, a species unfit for democracy.

Other countries cultivated charm, but you can't hoard charm, it's frittered away every time you have a chat. And what use does it have? Nothing but wasteful emotional frivolity, hardly a functioning waste-disposal service. Here, though, they're well versed at preserving anything devoid of charm. Functionality trumped charm.

They loathed foreigners who had an oily and knowing way of speaking, they hated them even more than the work-shy. They were suspicious of anyone who was quick on the uptake, inventive and precise at the same time, and so audacious as to flaunt it and occupy a senior position. Behind the dismissive mask, I discovered feelings of inferiority. This mask was a larva, a vulnerable larva in its developmental stage.

Even so, one group of people were fond of the foreign girls: vulnerable old ladies who were infirm and needy. We would offer them our seats on the tram, pick up coins they dropped, and Mara was once so bold as to open a door when she heard a faint moan from behind it. Her neighbour had fallen and was lying there. She called the ambulance. Mara had soon forgotten about her good deed, but it didn't come to nothing. The resurrected neighbour remembered Mara every Easter and showered her with money and chocolate.

In the stairwell of the psychiatric outpatient clinic hangs a work of art: large-meshed white cotton netting stretches across the stairwell, meandering up to the fifth floor. I climb the stairs and admire the metaphor: we're here to catch you.

In a windowless room a woman is sobbing. She doesn't want to be crying, she insists. She stares at the psychiatrist as if he's to blame.

'You can't control it.' He fends off her accusing glare.

'But why? Why do I get dizzy when I see full supermarket shelves? Why does it hurt so much when I hear noisy trams and loud voices?'

The young psychiatrist is a double, triple foreigner, his overloaded accent is composed of several languages. It takes some effort to peel the words away from his accent to make sense of them. The hospital is a large workshop with an international team of craftsmen. Here they're repairing a broken bone, there a twisted thought.

'Does everything seem unreal to you when you are in that state of mind?'

'It's real, Doctor!' she screams. 'Believe me!'

I manage to see comedy in her despair. That makes it easier to separate myself from the other person's unhappiness. I interpret with relish, I summarize the patient's rambling sentences, I become an ambassador for clarity.

'Are you having suicidal thoughts?' the psychiatrist asks casually, as if about a sniffly nose.

'But you're not going to lock me up?'

'No, no.'

The psychiatrist is a sometimes-amused, sometimes-dour spectator of a tragicomedy. But it's not theatre. It is a service to defuse confusion. Inside, he can chuckle at his patients' follies, and wearily tell his wife in the evenings as he flicks through the TV channels, 'Oh, I had another panic case again today.'

The patient remembers back to her previous strength. 'I was a car mechanic back home, I love the smell of petrol.'

The psychiatrist's eyes are suddenly alert. 'What's that? You were a car mechanic?'

'Yeah, and at the weekend I drove my Honda, I won races. But since I landed on my ear, the whistling and roaring has been driving me crazy, this wooh wooh wooh. I'm forgetting everything. Why do I keep forgetting things?'

'Your strength is absorbed by your fears, that's why.'

'Tell me, doctor, am I mentally ill, or is it the tinnitus?'

'The tinnitus was the trigger, then your anxieties seem to have developed a momentum of their own. They're mutually dependent.' He locks his fingers together and stands up. 'Now let's take a break, then we'll take a blood sample.'

'I forgot to say I got married.'

'Congratulations.'

'He says he loves me. I'm moving to the country with him. There's no tram there, maybe that will help with the vertigo.'

'Ah, definitely.'

Now the patient rushes at me, holds her tearful face close to my nose and complains with such force it's as if she were reporting on robbery, torture and murder. And it is robbery, torture, and murder. The invisible, cruel perpetrator can wreak havoc at any time, he'll trap her in the house, convince her that she's crazy and that no one's willing to help. The world is cruel.

I run down the stairs. No, the white nets are not a work of art. They're real. Safety nets for suicides.

If my neighbour ever wanted to borrow a scrubbing brush, she would initiate her bold request with a submissive 'Bitte' and conclude with a cascade of 'Mercidanke'. I would be wounded by her 'Bittemerci', as though she deemed me incapable of fulfilling the desires of the heart, quite besides the fact that I didn't possess any kind of scrubbing device. But no, she never came to borrow anything, I only wished she would. How could she as a housewife ever admit to misplacing her scrubbing brush?

'Bittemerci' echoed all around. This refrain of 'Bittemerci' made me sad, it was like a fence between us. If you're huddled up close enough together, no empty phrase can get in the way. It only spreads to fill the void of formality. Where had gratitude migrated to? It had been trumped by a platitude, its lifeless doppelgänger. Even tiny infants were hounded with refined injunctions, 'Please, stop it!' This constant 'Bittemerci' was a scrubbing brush that blurred the boundary between good and bad. Even your foe was treated to this mystical formula thought to summon peace out of thin air. Anyone facing rejection was told, in writing, and with respect and sincere regret, to kindly go to hell.

Some people suffered from a mania for greetings, acknowledging everyone they encountered, whether in the sauna or in the woodland undergrowth. 'Grüezi' wasn't the rolling stone that starts an avalanche. 'Grüezi' wasn't a yearning for intimacy. To respond with a playful interjection of their own was as bold an obstruction as a foot in the doorway. 'Grüezi' was nothing more than a DO NOT DISTURB! sign hanging on the door. Illiterate as I was, it took me years to learn to decipher these three words. They were the key to my host country. The key that could open no lock.

The locals didn't know that life was a struggle, they expected me, their placid fellow citizen, to murmur uniform apologies at their constant admonitions. If they unintentionally touched someone, they would apologize profusely. It was only in this apology that I discovered a kernel of passion. Was that why they apologized so often and so gladly? Apologies were the fabric softener of life. They were supposed to make human relationships smooth and supple. To cover all bases, best of all was a precautionary, 'Salü, exgüsi!' Hi, excuse me!

Instead of 'Close the window,' they said, 'Sorry, would you mind, could I trouble you? Would you be so kind as to please close the window? It's very good of you, merci, and have a lovely weekend.' And it wasn't enough to endure this vexatious torrent, you had to respond, 'Merci, and the same to you.' Any deviation was an affront to civilization and had polite society raging against me.

What linguistic luxury abounded here! For even prosaic, mundane matters, people indulged in a courtly language rich in subjunctives. Back home, there was an unseemly extension of the private into the public; here, officialese ate its way into the private sphere. However, they expended so much subjunctive energy that at some point they no longer had any subjunctivity left, no stamina for lofty concerns. If I preserved my energy for loftier matters and resorted to an efficient 'Shut the window!', the locals were reminded of the command, 'Ready, aim, fire!' Only the military had this primordial immediacy, free of contamination by diplomatic language.

In the airlock we put on yellow plastic coats and rubber gloves. The senior physician gives me a special protective mask, pressing it right up against my face. Then we enter the patient's room, where the air is filtered around the clock. And still a few employees get infected every year. We stand at a great distance from a small, slender man. So, this is the dangerous monster held in a cage for our protection. Solitary confinement has made him very docile. He arrived at the transit camp a week ago. In his country, he had contracted open tuberculosis from former prisoners.

'How are you feeling?' asks the doctor.

'Well. I quit smoking, I'm coughing and sweating less.'

'We'll start the treatment today. But the tuberculosis bacteria are resistant. They don't give up easily.'

'Do I have holes in my lungs?'

'Holes, you could call them that. And you have hepatitis C. That's from a contaminated syringe. That wouldn't have been possible in our hospital.'

'I know. Everything is possible in my country.'

He isn't fleeing war, nor is he a political activist. He doesn't make up a story of persecution and he doesn't complain. Why should he? He's come to the right place. This empty room is the promised land. From here the only possible routes are towards death or a future.

He points to the dictionary lying open on the bedside table and says the most important word in this foreign language: 'Danke.' Thank you.

'You're in good hands here,' I say to the man as I leave. 'Get well soon.'

In the airlock, the doctor mumbles as he takes off his face mask.

'He knows he'll die if left untreated. Hopefully they won't deport him in the middle of treatment. Then everything would have been pointless.'

'How could that happen if moving him poses a fatal threat to anyone in his vicinity?'

'You're right. They can only move him if we can reduce the risk posed by the bacteria. But it's likely that the medication won't have any impact.'

On the way home I imagine myself, behind the protective face mask, interpreting the unfortunate man's last words on his deathbed. If the alternative possibility comes about, however, he will probably be the happiest refugee ever to be deported.

*As a linguistic emergency service, I twist and turn in languages
like roaming in winding streets, brushing someone's arm as I
pass, catching someone's eye. These are disturbing journeys.
The first time I meet a client I'm curious about their problem,
the second time the pattern deepens, by the third time it's
become repetitive, the fourth time it's annoying, the fifth time
it wears me down and gradually, by the sixth time, I report to
the interpreting centre that my head is spinning. Vertigo is a
common work-related complaint. At that point, a colleague
steps onto the language carousel in my place.*

Something strange happened. Femininity threw itself over me,
covered me completely. And it was this—my femininity—and
not me that was seen. I was met with approving looks on the
street, and when I entered a room, my appearance was an
event. Rumour had it that I was aloof. But I wasn't unap-
proachable, it was just the beauty that so many found intimi-
dating, like a female bodyguard. An angel had come down to
help me in my great need, a compensation for my foreignness,
but also an amplification of it. This femininity was foreignness
personified. It lent me sharp contours that distinguished me
from the others. In my country I wouldn't have needed any
sharpness, society would have blurred the edges, would never
have let any contours emerge. I wouldn't have got these big,
melancholy eyes, green irises half disappearing against their
white background under the upper eyelid. And yet they saw
more than they were allowed. Being foreign ground me to a

polish like a goldsmith. In the summer I swam butterfly and dressed in such a way that this beauty could surface, my homage to my rescuer, this femininity that let me live in dignity. She carried me with a lascivious gait. Sometimes I thought she was me and I was her. But I knew that one day we would part.

Mara said that female beauty had it tough, in dictatorship and democracy alike. It's endangered everywhere, she argued, and the state should set up a special ministry to protect it, with officials, and soldiers and Alsatians, an authority as imposing and important as the Ministry of Defence. Because 'Beautiful girls are important,' Mara insisted. If our foreign looks put some men off seeking access, others saw it as a free pass. Men of all ages, every shoe size and no matter what intelligence quotient staked their claim with a glance, a whistle, a word, a gesture, and a grope. Some begged like junkies to be allowed to touch us, the rich drug baronesses who could score them a hit. It was disgusting, frightening and amazing to discover what our looks could do. We were accused of negligence, of depravity, of tantalizing them with gifts we weren't prepared to give. We weren't trying to tantalize, we were tantalizing.

I quickly turned the rules of the game to my advantage. I was desired, which meant I had value. This girl who had shot up tall with uneven breasts—one full and round like a woman's, the other still puny and pointy—had an unexpected gain in power. No one had even seen her bare chest and already they were scarred by the sight. An accolade for courage and a souvenir of pain. Excursions into the outside world were battles, I came under fire from other people's longings. An old man asked me for help, I went into his house, and shakily he pushed me onto the bed. I escaped screaming. And the teacher stared at my mouth as I reeled off irregular verbs, he lost his balance and clung to my neck. I shook him off like a cockchafer. Should I shake off this beauty too, stamp it into the ground and erect a wooden cross on it? Gingerly I felt my body and asked myself what the others wanted from me and with what right. Would I be safe if I spurned the gift of femininity and draped myself in rags?

Instead, I refused to let myself be deprived of what was mine and I went on the attack. If I went to a party, my eyes skimmed over all the female guests. Like a mafia boss making sure no one was contesting his turf. Phew, there was no one more beautiful than me. Oh no, there was one, she was my match. Our eyes met. We recognized each other as members of a secret society, we each approached the other. I needed backup. Mara and I, together we were invincible. As we walked along the riverfront, there was a silent cheer from the benches and cafes. The refugee girls had arrived, a triumph over the social hierarchy. Their glances swept us up. And already we dreamed of visiting our beauty upon the cities. No metropolis was safe from us, we would conquer. The local girls, with their affluent circumstances and modest bodies, pooh-poohed our idiotic ambition. They shuddered to see us expose ourselves. This wasn't hard work, it was theatre, a frivolous game. Idle pursuits were frowned upon, drudgery was revered, beauty was exhorted to tone itself down, get down on its knees. Just no showing off—that would be unfair on your fellow citizens.

We weren't happy. The melancholy did its work. Our tragic mistress was in charge. Our style was broken. For us there was always martial law. We sent out our troops and didn't hide our foreignness. It was our Achilles heel and our trump card. We tarted our foreignness up in bright fabrics from thrift stores. Look, hardship can have its pluses. It caused us no end of outrage. We zealously heaped up envy and traded it for self-respect. We showed what we had, saved nothing for later. There was a hunger for validity, there was only the here and now. We didn't want to be spectators in life, we despised restraint. A fun fair atmosphere, itinerant artistes, fanfares and feats of their own making. A tightrope walk. Arrogance gave us balance. We never crash-landed. But it was a close shave, a hundred times a day.

There she comes in her translucent skirt, hemmed with red ruffles, like sexy lingerie. Half of her bosom peeks out from a red camisole—the words 'red' and 'beautiful' are related in her language. Her heavy body tapers into red patent-leather shoes, threatening to crush them. She complains that she's persecuted by a compulsive idea, the sense that passers-by are laughing at her. Her clothes can't hold her body back from overflowing, and her words bubble up, revealing her most intimate side. She's been left naked since several men raped her. In her dreams she sees her murdered husband packing up the furniture and carrying it out of their shared apartment. Her soul empties itself, the dead man carries out the soul's contents. Back then, after finding traces of violence on his corpse, she went in search of his murderers. Her husband was a big shot and political circles warned her not to push for answers. She didn't give up and that's when they gave her a warning. Taught her a lesson that has changed her life forever.

The psychiatrist is also a foreigner here, he has an oval face and green eyes. His chosen manner of politeness is mischievous and lithe, his eloquence impressive. I swing myself deftly up to a higher linguistic level and am delighted to find that I interpret with presence of mind, vigilantly selecting elegant formulations. These are my language gifts for him.

'Doctor, my eyes can't help looking for the cognac bottle in the supermarket. I know it's crazy with all the medication.'

'We can't control everything. Illogical desires arise in us from the depths. Control is useful, but only eighty per cent. If we don't sin, no one can forgive us.'

What to do with the desire that rises in me from the depths? I try with all my might to bring it under control. And here is a specialist of the soul saying that I should sin, that he would forgive me. His answers are meant for me too, especially for me. At the same time, I know that I am the interpreter here and that I am imagining the ambiguity. I can no longer look at the psychiatrist, I feel exposed, my forbidden thoughts are visible to him. Life is bulging, bursting free, something overpowering is happening.

'Doctor, if my husband visits me in a dream, someone will die.'

'Have you checked?' he asks. 'Has anyone died yet?'

She draws a breath. 'Tomorrow I'm going to cardiology to hear my death sentence.'

The psychiatrist argues against it, but the patient doesn't want to be deprived of her tragedies, the medals that life has bestowed upon her. You become somebody when you experience tragedy. Now she plays the self-hatred trump card.

'Doctor, when I look at myself in the mirror, I want to give myself a slap.'

'You should look for ways to give yourself the space to find pleasure.'

Is he saying that he's contemplating finding pleasure with me? The patient fades away with her whining, she's just our matchmaker. I am threatened with a loss of reality. Does he see that and is he treating me too? No, he has stepped out of the psychiatrist role and is flirting away. A male omnipotence fantasy with two women dependent on him at the same time. Perhaps it's happening to him too, like me, one subconscious speaking tenderly to another. Twenty per cent of uncontrollable desires fly back and forth, filling the high-ceilinged room of the old building of the psychiatric clinic.

Our intimacy needs a third party. I am the centre where the threads come together. He only knows half of what I say, the other half remains concealed from him, as if I were half veiled and lay half in the dark. I could cheat. He has to trust me. That trust is love. I caress his words, which I transform into another language, and bring him gifts of new words, decorating them like a bridal wreath. I am gripped by fear that

*the patient might recover or kill herself or be deported and I
would never see the psychiatrist again.*

*'Doctor,' the patient complains, 'when I go out on the
street, I don't dare look at anyone.'*

*'Looking away costs you energy. I'm setting you home-
work. Look one passer-by in the eye every day. Let that person
take the burden from you.'*

*I prevail over myself, I look the psychiatrist in the eye, dive
into the green pond and become weightless.*

*When saying goodbye, he says to me, 'I took on this case
because I've never treated a patient via an interpreter. It's
an interesting experience. I shall write an academic paper
about it.'*

I took a lover, I met a new nation. A laid-back way of walking,
wildly gesticulating arms, thick accents and subtle ones, different skin tones, the inner limp of the uprooted people of all
countries. It could be just a word, a look of recognition, and
I would be hit by the warmth that flowed from other people's
foreignness. I found acceptance in our common difference, I
could drift in the waters of the unknown. A language with a
thousand accents became our father tongue. Exempted from
the duty of polite acquiescence towards our host country, we
sneered at it and mocked it; we told tall tales, tricking ourselves, exaggerating beyond all measure, hitting the bull's eye,
our laughter resounding as we walked away with a wave.

Among ourselves, nobody could hit back with that dreaded phrase, 'If you don't like it, just go back home.'

I had found it: the land of whingeing. I had found a new *us*. There it was, that freedom of expression. With no guarantee in law, we experienced it underground, just as in the dictatorships we had fled. We ate from the forbidden fruits of blasphemous realization, long since expelled from paradise. A whirlwind of hurt feelings and hostile thoughts simmered, an immigrant insurrection that bubbled up but never quite broke through the polished surface. It was a protest never brought to fruition; it was never to be seen on the podiums or TV screens. When approached by a local, we fell silent as though a secret agent were listening. We put on a harmless expression, our well-versed camouflage.

The nation of foreigners resided here with no audible voice.

'We are here!' we should have announced. 'You need to reckon with us, with our otherness. We don't want to emulate you; not everything you have is worth copying. And it is impossible to be grateful long term. That would be artificial, but we want authenticity.'

If only we had emerged from the underground and invited the locals to a national celebration. Opened up to them with everything we knew, everything we worried and made a fuss about, our legitimate demands and our desires. But who would have wanted to listen to us in this thankless foreign country? We immigrants were an ununified people, disorganized, unrevolutionary, enfeebled by our sense of inferiority, insecure in our new language, cowering before our adopted rules, plagued by homesickness, willing to adapt even at the expense of our dignity, united and mutinous only in our covert grumbling.

Amidst all the slander, someone pipes up. 'But not everyone's like that. I know someone . . .' The closed front is undermined, defectors emerge who move between worlds. Occasionally, locals are swept up in the multi-ethnic stream, they're also only native by gradual weathering, after all.

Outsiders, strangers in their own country came to us and said, 'It's good that you're here. We were pushed off the tightrope by our compatriots. You were there to catch our fall.'

The mental iron curtain I had clung to had disappeared long before the actual one was dismantled. Dialogues emerged, but they didn't bubble up like the homely porridge in the magic pot.

I passed a lady as I cycled by on the pavement. This time I didn't get a threatening glare but a smile. Who was she? And who did she think I was? The other foreigners were starting to think I was a local, offering me excessive thanks and preemptive apologies for even being here. When I outed myself as a foreigner, we would laugh, laughing at the ludicrous notion of there being locals and foreigners.

Among the immigrant population, too, all were not equal. We were a tribal society of ethnic groups. There was an established pecking order, where those who had been here for some time looked down on the newcomers. I refused to let myself be categorized by ethnicity: 'My name is Emigrazia. My home is being a foreigner. I won't let myself be emigrated from here.'

Back then, before the wedding, she warned him:

'I'm fifteen years older than you. Do you want to drag this old sack around with you?'

But for him, this sack was full of jewels. She had been a goldsmith who had lived in the big cities of the world. She examined fine gemstones with her magnifying glass while he drove around his homeland with a truck full of shingle. He was only too happy to leave the dusty country roads and curl up inside her massive folds, until he was lost in her, this boulder of hundred and twenty kilograms.

He shifts her from the bed to the wheelchair, and from there he heaves her onto the toilet, nudging her big belly from the side until it hangs low over the toilet bowl between her legs. She passes water and has a bowel movement on the way. This is what he calls 'turbulent times', when he has to wipe everything down, wash the bedclothes; everything has to be spic and span for him. She has diabetes, artificial heart valves and an open ulcer on her leg that has festered for months.

'Real elephant legs,' he chuckles.

He gets dizzy when he lifts her leg. This is because of the narrowed artery in his neck. He's also got asthma, haemor-rhoids, oh yes, a torn ligament, an inflamed jaw and bowel problems; he has to wear an incontinence pad when he leaves the house. He's the carer, but he is ill, too.

The doctor tries to pick through the sack of woes that the patient empties at his feet, working out which are his, which are hers, and since when. But the man no longer knows where his body ends. He injects his wife with insulin for the last time *at 3 a.m., then falls asleep in their marital bed. Early in the morning, he responds to her groan of pain, cleans up the ulcerous wound on her leg. Then it's time to cook, quickly do the shopping, give her another shot of insulin, in-between elaborate trips to the toilet, until finally it's evening and time for* Who Wants to Be a Millionaire? *on TV. When his work is done, knowing his wife is next to him, clean and fed, he's left feeling almost carefree. She teases him. 'You dozed off in front of the television!' He laughs.*

'How do you feel knowing your wife is at home on her own for two hours?'

'Awful. What if she gets diarrhoea, how is she going to get to the bathroom?'

He reports his physical exertion without disgust and without any rebellion. Because 'She needs me.'

It's only when he mentions a psychologist's recommendation to take a few weeks of holiday that any anger surfaces. She spouted some nonsense about how everyone has the right to only look after themselves.

'And how is that supposed to work?'

The couple has long since curled up in their nest of diseased flesh, accepting the bare minimum of external professional physical care; nurses come into the house, but he doesn't appreciate their help. He doesn't want to be deprived of his sole authority.

He learned early on that people exist to be there for others. Of the nine children his mother gave birth to, three died in infancy. She gave birth to twins out in the field, and although she quickly got the girls warming up in the stove, they died of pneumonia. Then he was born, and another brother came every year after him. The children had chores in the house and on the farm, while the mother dragged sacks of potatoes about. Once she came home sad, he asked what was going on, and he was slapped in the face for asking. That's how he found out about the death of his youngest sister. Then the time of babies was over, the father fell into the brook when he was drunk and froze to death. No, he doesn't drink. He took his mother's values to heart. His devotion could support a whole horde of children. But it's illnesses that are his babies. They never grow up and leave home, but year after year they get new siblings.

The family doctor has applied for a disability certificate, but he proudly stands up to the doctor who examines him.

'I'm one hundred per cent fit for work. Caring for my wife is a full job.'

Although I wish I could hand him a surgical knife that could sever him from his own self-destruction, I say the opposite, paying tribute to his social value: 'You're a good person.'

'Oh no, it's what anyone would do.'

Feigning a modest brush-off is part of the culture of self-abandonment, which still rests deep within me and which he has now awakened. I don't lead him to the sharp scalpel that could save him, that I only learned about in exile. And his eyes thank me with a happy glow.

Surveillance was part and parcel of living here. The country was one big secret archive. Nothing was ever to disappear. Everything that happened was painstakingly recorded, catalogued, filed away. Voluntary archivists bustled about all over the place. The probing questions started the moment I opened my mouth.

'When did it happen? Where was it? Who was present? What was his name?'

I might say something about the mood, how I felt: pointless contributions.

'Stick to the facts, miss.'

It wasn't the same, though, if I requested specific information. If I asked what their salary was—back home, a key question that demonstrated genuine interest—they would raise their eyes and give a response both vague and evasive:

'Enough.'

In this national archive, everything had a place and a name. And the more impersonal the interaction, the more people insisted on being addressed by name.

'Miss X doesn't greet her neighbours by name,' it would say in my naturalization file, if I dared say hello without addressing my neighbour personally. 'Insufficient assimilation.'

If you don't know someone's name, you don't belong; you're uncouth and foreign. These terms were interchangeable. But as much as I tried, I could never get my head around the name Rüdisühli. I would never forget the kind neighbourly look, though.

Mara was more resourceful in this respect. After every 'Adieu, Frau' she would mumble something and round it off with a -*li*. Thanks to this stroke of genius, she was entrusted with a red passport that got her waved through every border crossing.

There was another repeat offence I was accused of.

'Miss X has neglected the snow shovelling again this winter.'

Corrupted by a dictatorship where the state was responsible for everything, I had mistakenly believed that snow was common property. In fact, it was a private burden entrusted to me personally.

I possessed a stateless passport. If I wanted to cross a border, I was directed to customs. My blue pass would be examined suspiciously. No state took responsibility for me. I had one square metre to stand on. The only solid ground I had was myself. I shovelled and swept free the spot on which I stood, and in another shameless provocation I claimed not to remember which day was my laundry day. This helped attract recruits to xenophobic groups.

The naturalization detectives were on the prowl. 'If you see Miss X standing in front of the house, do you get the impression that she's a local?'

'Oh no,' answered my neighbour. Later, he tried to justify himself to me: 'Well, I could hardly have lied to the gentlemen.'

A panel of serious-looking men of various professions and a housewife gathered in a school to grill me on how democracy worked, asking if I knew who held the reins of power in this just and fair society. As if I could fail to notice. The head of the naturalization committee lamented, 'You have been critical of our country.'

'Because I'm a good citizen.'

The jury pronounced its verdict. 'The naturalization application cannot be approved.'

But I didn't give up. I had been here for years by now, I had made friends, and their signatures witnessed my successful assimilation. 'Assimilation' sounds like melting away. I would have preferred them to have confirmed my participation, but the idea that immigrants should be allowed to participate in society while remaining as themselves was a bold one back then.

When it was finally time to be ceremonially blessed by the gift of mercy, the naturalization official decreed, 'You'll all be happy and grateful to hold our passport.'

People from many countries sat there politely, and nobody stood up to add, 'And you'll be happy and grateful that we came to live here.'

But at some point, someone has to make a stand. They lumped 'Miss' in front of my mutilated name, making me the least interesting person I knew, that is, I didn't know her at all. I went to court to win my name back: the feminine ending the border guard had stolen from me when I arrived in the country. But my new no-frills homeland didn't want to give me back my chopped-off diacritics, so I made a point of adding them back in myself, every time I wrote my name. There I was: myself again.

The courtroom, which sees a lot of coming and going, is grubby. The air is stale, the carpet, the wooden chairs and the long tables are worn out, only the alleged thief is defiant, throbbing with life. He's the heart of the action, after all. He stands in the middle of the room. The judge asks, in an unduly sombre tone, whether the accused knew the name of the meat that he was accused of stealing. The tall young man doesn't know and insists that he didn't steal it, that it was the other guy, who fled the scene. When the judge reads from the thick file, he translates from the standard language into the local dialect. In doing so, he's saying, we've lived here the longest, this is our home, we make the rules.

'You have a criminal record.'

'That's in the past. I'm a different person now.'

His trendy look, his gelled-up hairstyle, doesn't exactly help him fit in.

'Why do you carry pliers with you?'

'Is it against the law? Are pliers a weapon?'

The judge sighs. 'Pliers are sometimes used to remove the security tags from products.'

The young man is equipped for pickpocketing. The judge sees the reason for this in his childhood.

'I know you've had a hard time. Your mother died in childbirth, you lost your father in the war.'

The detective from the supermarket timidly declares under oath that she saw with her own eyes how the defendant stuffed two kilos of lamb into his backpack.

The judge gives a concerned nod and issues his verdict.

'Seven days in prison.'

The defendant throws himself on his knees and spreads his arms. 'I'm innocent! I swear by my mother!' Then he remembers that he's declared her dead. 'By her memory.'

The judge and the clerk each take two steps back. The detective cowers in the corner. The usual order is disrupted by a theatricality that people here only know from novels. I step closer to the guy. He rushes into my arms, sobbing, and I pat his shoulder with a reassuring laugh.

'Oh, little paws, that's nothing. Just seven days.'

Soon after, he apologises for the tears.

'What did you call him?' the judge asks me.

'Little paws'

'Aha, thief,' he says, reassured.

'No, "little paws" is a term of endearment, like "sweetheart".'

At that, he takes two steps back.

We leave the courthouse, and the young man looks to me not just for tactile but for moral support.

'The refugee home is full of enemies, the ones we were at war with. It's unbearable. They killed my father.'

'And what was your father doing in their country? He killed others, too.'

'That was an order.'

'You can refuse an order.'

'Refuse an order?'

This defiant spirit utters the monstrous idea out loud and takes three steps back.

The locals loved treating foreigners to their dialects, tempting them with one vernacular dish after another. They led us from valley to valley, from the home farm of one accent to another. Here the dialect was a terse, jagged landscape of unfamiliar guttural sounds. This way of speaking didn't prance about gaily on a parquet dance floor; it knew nothing of the indolence and elegance that derives from such luxury. Should I kick off my patent-leather shoes? It was a different life experience to mine that was coded in the dialects of these steep valleys. I wasn't some placid summer visitor, enjoying their quaint rural lilt; I had been condemned to settle here. The dialect was the clan's territorial marker, its characteristic scent. If you didn't smell of the dialect, you were a rotten outsider. They didn't see you as a foreign guest bringing incense from afar. The dialects knew nothing of flight for the sake of flying; the only motion they knew was earthy traction. Immigrants struggled in vain to add something of themselves to the dialect, to create neologisms that would expand them and the world inch by inch.

I only cared for the written language, the formal, standard language that smelled of nothing: a tall, empty, whitewashed house, with many floors, spacious rooms and lofty ceilings. That was where I wanted to set myself up, where I would host linguistic balls. Many locals were suspicious of their standard language: it didn't come from down here, from the guts. For them, it was abstract and antiseptic. And for me too, it was a language of the head. It didn't resonate through my whole body like a mother tongue. In the *Hochsprache*, the 'high language', my voice squeaked like a castrato. I tried to lure it down a pitch, but it stuck to its soaring heights.

The new language was the greatest adventure of exile, and I spared no effort to explore it. It was more than my survival as a linguistic being that was at stake, I wanted my linguistic dignity. Speaking the standard language was my way of saying, 'The dialects are yours. I'll learn to understand them, but I'm not going to speak them.' Just as they left my gift of their *Hochsprache* unopened in the corner, so did I with their dialects. What a tragic marriage of tongues we had! Sometimes I doubted myself. I was embarrassed by my linguistic approach, crippled by shame, but I battled against it, reassuring myself, 'It's not the language that connects us, but what it conveys.' When someone spoke loudly in dialect, I would sometimes run away, as if I could escape the homelessness that pursued me. I could not and did not want to belong, so I would forever stand apart. It was exhausting defending the castle of my language identity day in, day out. But in this vast, pure solitude the standard language flourished.

At the start of a conversation, they would politely ask you, 'Do you understand dialect?'

Rather than answering with a docile yes, I preferred to turn it around, so I was dealing out the cards. 'Shall we revel in your formal language?'

From time to time someone would accept my invitation to join these orgies of ill repute, and we would twirl around the parquet dance floor until we were dizzy, drunk on the lexical intoxication. But my dance partner's light steps would be met with his countrymen's contempt. The warm stables of hospitality were only open to anyone who mouthed the sounds of the formal tongue with gruff reluctance. And what an outrage, if a foreigner deigned to close herself off, to build herself a linguistic fortress. Would I be trapped with an eternal stammer? I held out a mirror to show them their own disability, and they pushed me away: 'Don't you miss your native language? Don't you want to return to it?'

So, I kept my ideas about language to myself. It was too early to speak out. But I lived them. Emigration doesn't mean swapping your ancestral community for any old thing that comes along. Emigrazia is flexible, elastic, permeable. And that's how her language should be.

Mara couldn't hold out against the pressure, she began to break into dialect. That was the linguistic junction where we went our separate ways. It wasn't out of the joy of discovery that Mara followed this path, she simply made the decision to arrive. For me, it meant toadying to the locals and that hurt. Bumbling along in the standard language means walking with one's head held high, even with a limp; it's a public confession of being foreign. But Mara wanted to hide this fact, seeking camouflage in the dialect.

For fifteen years she fussed around women's heads, her speech flowed without thought like the water with which she washed their hair. But sometimes her words were as sharp as her scissors. She wasn't going to let the tough life out there knock her off her feet. The hair salon was the place of her self-affirmation. Then she responded to a tempting marriage proposal in the newspaper small ads. A car mechanic, twenty years her senior, he looked serious in the photo. 'Do you want a new father?' she asked her son. 'Then get ready.' And they took the train, travelling for two days and two nights, to the land of dreams.

'I was a person, now I'm nobody.'

She is still someone, a wild mother beast, who senses her child is in danger and uses her racing speech to defend herself. Her thin arms slice the air, her eyes bore into the school psychologist.

'I'm not here to judge you,' says the psychologist, correcting her assumption. 'My job is to protect your son. Why is he habitually absent from school?'

'He gets up in the morning, looks at me, and I can see it. I ask, have you got a migraine again? And he sinks back into bed.'

'He has hardly any muscle.'

'But he can walk to the bus station.'

'The school isn't keen to take him back.'

'He's not aggressive, he does what he's told. I do my duty, my child is always clean and well fed.'

'Is there something wrong in the family?'

'It's the hole inside my husband. He fills it up with alcohol every night. My son gets a stomach ache just seeing him.'

The woman is highly strung, burning through her last reserves of fat. The boy piles on fat to insulate against electric shocks. He's put on eighteen kilos since arriving in this foreign land.

'In half a year he hasn't learned to say a single entire sentence in our language,' says the psychologist. 'That suggests resistance. He doesn't want to stay here.'

The woman shudders, you can almost hear her bones rattle. But it's just the metal of her necklace against her flat chest.

'My child needs me now more than ever.'

'You're an overprotective mother.'

The woman is speechless. So, a mother's love is bad?

'In her culture, the relationship between mother and son can be very close,' I say, advocating for empathy. 'Even closer than between a married couple.'

The woman concurs, folding her arms like wings. And as if remembering that certain birds take turns to care for their brood, she adds, 'If only my husband would pay him some attention. But he only knows one parenting method: sports and military drills.'

'You should create small islands for yourself. Go to a cafe, have a chat with a friend.'

'But I talk to my sister on Skype for hours on end. Otherwise, I would have gone mad here long ago.'

The local calls out from the mainland to the woman drowning out at sea: 'Small islands!'

And the capsized child is floating on a raft of fat.

The woman goes to meet some others from her country and hears grim contemporary fairy tales of men starving their imported brides to force them to obey, even selling them to other men, to finance their drug addictions. They make her own husband seem like a philanthropist.

But the boy carries on being truant from school. He surfs the internet all day.

The school psychologist fights her way past the drunk man and his barking pit bull, and enters the boy's room.

'If you were a wizard, what would you conjure up?'

'I would put the bad man in a hat and make him disappear.'

'What does the bad man do?'

'He yells at me and hits the dog.'

The boy kisses a kitten on the nose and wraps it around his neck as though it were the flexible part of his own immobile body. The cat tears itself away and scratches the door, longing to be let out, but the pit bull is waiting in the corridor. The woman doesn't know how they can both get out of this trap. If she gets a divorce, she'll be deported. A disgrace. She can already picture the malicious stares.

'If you want to stay here, you need to tackle three things: an apartment, the language, a job,' explains the psychologist.

'I warn you, it won't be easy to get settled here. My compatriots have a square soul.'

'My mother is strong as a cockroach,' says the boy.

'A cockroach at home and a cockroach abroad are not the same thing,' says the psychologist.

The boy strokes the cat for two hours, both of them needy, a craving to be touched. Now he kisses his mother, a long and ardent kiss. A fourteen-year-old who's secured the easiest of all forms of love. And a woman swaps her independence for a marriage that renders her powerless. Just because the doss house she's ended up in is in a rich country. Did she think she was going to marry the country? Bluebeard has already lured another ten brides here before her. He stays true to his taste— they were all from the same country. Only one managed to endure the marriage long enough to get a residence permit.

When he's drunk, the husband starts beating his eleventh wife.

'Go to the police,' he sneers. 'It'll only speed up your deportation.'

She comforts herself with a word of solace from her mother, grandmother and all her loved ones. It can be translated in two ways: 'Sit it out' or 'Suck it up'.

Everything neatly separated: emotions from rational thinking, work life from private life, church from state. Only the economy and the military were a melting pot of faith. Once a year,

our neighbour did his few weeks' service as a decorated briga-
dier. Whether he was an ordinary fusilier with a hand grenade
or operating an anti-tank guided missile, he shouldn't even
have been allowed to command the pharma industry's lab
rats. One career here, another career there, the one not existing without the other. When his son called for secularization,
his enraged father sent him packing, to the evil empire, no
less—that's what he called it, where I was from. 'And make it
a one-way ticket!'

Of course, I preferred the son. We both had insufferable
fathers, and we might almost have become accomplices if the
son hadn't just transfigured my dictatorship into the kingdoms
of the good. I was politically stigmatized, a traitor who had
abandoned his utopia. Only amnesia could render me worthy
of his affection. I was just discovering the blessings of democracy and here he was experimenting with a closed system. It
wasn't reality that he craved but rebellion against his father.
Polar opposites in black and white. They didn't need my
colourful experience.

I heard about a young writer who called himself Zorn,
anger. He had penned his reckoning with the Gold Coast,
exposing the coldness of its inhabitants. The lack of love on
the coast was the executioner who would finish him off.
But he wouldn't accept his death sentence, to be carried out
in the form of cancer, he would rebel. He still hoped for a cure
by naming the cruelty he had suffered. His real name was
Angst—*fear*—but it was as Zorn that he described his childhood and youth amid the terrible poverty of the rich. I was
shaken by his book. This was a local revealing the truth in a

more radical way than any foreigner. I found my own nebulous thoughts articulated to a clear and painful conclusion, and beyond. Zorn linked the Gold Coast with his cancer. He awoke in me the courage to think beyond the sheepish whispers. The relentless critic wasn't thrown in jail, but meted out a different fate. I wasn't interested in whether it was true or not that it was the Gold Coast that was killing him. Zorn had conceived of the rich as his executioners, and he had dared to speak out. His dark wrath gave me clarity of vision. Zorn became my lucky charm.

As I delved deeper into the essence of this country, I realized that not only was the local insistence on maintaining distance in every situation making me ill, but also that here illness wasn't met with comforting hugs and sent to bed, like at home, it wasn't cursed like a dictatorial regime, and the white pills were neither glorified nor condemned. With this most precious illness, you didn't crawl away into a symbiosis like it was a cosy habitat. It was neither fate nor force of nature, nor was it God's punishment. Strong words like this didn't summon up much sympathy. It was unseemly to use your illness to prevail over others. It was an inconspicuous citizen, its power curtailed like a despot by a constitution. Dissected under the microscope of thought, it shrivelled to the size of an equal life partner and I was sent off on my way with my clinical condition for company and encouraged to try and look for small solutions. Since my headache accompanied me wherever I went, I was curious to decipher its language.

It was the wall that had so often been held up against me that in the end proved to be my salvation. The culture of demarcation had always rejected my attempts to blur the boundaries. Wounded, I fled to my inner world, where I nurtured and preserved my personality. Outside, there were no exciting upheavals and disasters that needed my intervention. Instead, I cultivated the commotion within. I suddenly understood what a certain local writer meant when he said, 'Be humane, keep your distance.' I, too, was allowed to exercise the right to distance, I didn't need to assimilate myself. From now on, I was no longer in a forced marriage with my host country. This distance was well suited to thinking, indeed it was a prerequisite for it. In the cool shade of this wall stood a hard school bench, where I swotted away and occasionally found someone to talk to. I no longer relied on anyone accepting me. Still my effusive feelings flowed, but I directed the stream to where it was valued. Sometimes I opened the floodgates, sometimes I held back the flow. This dam was mine to control and the cabin atop the dam was my throne.

'What does my son need school for?' the father sneers. 'A man needs to be able to shoot, not know his ABC.'

The young psychologist nods serenely as though nothing of humankind is beyond her understanding. Then she turns briskly to the son.

'You beat up the other students pretty badly. The school management wants to have you excluded.'

The fifteen-year-old has a dull look. Such is his role in the presence of his father. To be lively or animated would be *tantamount to rebellion against the paternal authority. Instead of strength, the son chooses insight, a quality acquired in this foreign country.*

'I have a problem. If I don't react when someone insults me, I get obsessed with this feeling that I haven't seen things through. It's only when I punch someone that I can relax.'

The psychologist speaks softly now. 'Some non-violence training will teach you how the rules work here.'

'I know the rules, I want to learn how to see things through without breaking the rules.'

The father becomes suspicious. The son speaks the foreign language easily and quickly, he's too clever when he speaks, too soft, he's inching closer to the host country, away from the country of his forefathers. The son has become a battlefield, the site of a struggle between the traditional clan and modernity.

The father brings in the big war guns. 'As asylum seekers, we're treated here like the bottom of the heap. We have been waiting for a decision from the Migration Office for years. Call that respect? You and your asylum policy are to blame for my son's aggression.'

'But your son has a good chance of learning a trade after school.'

'Learning a trade's not what's important. A man needs to be able to defend himself, if necessary to the death.'

The father is a disaster. He has neither learned the language nor does he have a job. He puffs himself up, blustering and noisily claiming space that he couldn't occupy by peaceful means.

The psychologist persists in her formal courtesy. 'Do you consent to us applying for this training for your son?'

He sees the question as a weakness, and his tirade of hate becomes even bolder.

I want nothing more than to get away from here, I have to act.

'Of course he agrees,' I say. 'Give him the form to sign.'

The father signs, threatening, 'Nobody's getting their hands on my son!'

A year later, his anger has given way to a depression that makes for more pleasant interpreting. Grief—anger's older sister. But the enemy projection is still there.

'You people have made me ill, so help me get back on my feet. At home I was a free man, here everyone's always telling me what to do.'

'Learn the language and get a job, then you'll be free again,' I say, offering him simplistic advice from an integration brochure. His clumsy resistance is annoying, and all too familiar.

'It's easy for you to talk, you are strong-willed.'

These languageless foreigners are happy to rent this weakness. They jealously guard their only possession. The more

*strength they see in me, the more they hope to break off a
bit of it for themselves. They complain and complain. Then
they ask for my phone number. I have given it to two of my
favourite refugees, even though the rules of conduct for inter-
preters forbid it. Supposedly for our own protection.*

*'We have to adapt,' I tell the man, startled at myself. How
often have I heard this sentence from the locals, how often
have I raged against it?*

*'I was damaged by the war, and you of all people should
understand. But you're already on their side.'*

*'You're looking for a health resort, but you won't find it
here. This is real life.'*

At one event, I dismantled a politician's web of lies. But then
I was the one put in the dock, accused of whingeing. But it
had long ceased to be whingeing, it was a well-founded enu-
meration of grievances. I had learned to take vague distrust
and build it into a solid house of arguments, stone by stone.
The judge went through the charges as though she were climbing upstairs, floor after floor. But then she acquitted me of the
charge of libel. I fervently adored her sobriety, her factual
fidelity. I had a new-found respect for this method which had
once seemed so tedious to me, and I saw that behind her sever-
ity lay an endless warmth. It was a clear and soothing austerity
that knew how to disperse the fog of lies. On behalf of society,
the judge gave me the right to publicly expose the plaintiff's
lies and to denounce all lies. This was an essential part of

democracy, she stressed. I had become a pillar of democracy with my whingeing! And in this judge, I loved this country where I learned to sculpt my whingeing into solid form. You got no credit here, but work well done was given just reward. It's through what I've accomplished in my work that I've settled here, in this country for grown-ups. This is how I came to grow up: it was in the courtroom, in the ritual of right and wrong, that I adopted a fatherland. I had had to leave my motherland, but it lived on in me, I never lost it. I was the child of my parents, but also a cross of two cultures who kept crossing more barriers.

By then, I had long avoided the Two Confederates, the pub where my compatriots met to swap news and gossip. I steered clear of this constricting way of bouncing off one another emotionally, without thinking, and oh, the intrigues. In this microcosm, people tended to look at a female compatriot up and down, from top to bottom. The strength we had inherited—wit, ridicule, derision, irony—sometimes became a compulsion. Even our black humour had its iron rules, which a woman from our parts had to follow. Her laugh, her clothes, her lifestyle—all this gave her away as someone from the old country. They were never completely satisfied, there was always a 'but' . . . Was I supposed to feel guilty in the face of their eternal reproach, as though every step of my life meant me turning away from my roots? My path had led me away from where I had started out. I was more comfortable with foreigners whose customs I didn't know and to which I wasn't tied. They appreciated every gesture of sympathy, since they didn't feel entitled to it. With other foreigners, I felt refreshingly foreign.

I initially gave the benefit of the doubt to those who shared my mother tongue, but that was soon exhausted. When push came to shove, I was no longer corruptible. Another common ground took priority. My compatriots who had learned this vital life lesson abroad granted me the amulet of foreignness. Whenever we met, we were both foreign and familiar at the same time. No other kind of closeness was possible.

I started crossing borders to gather even more foreign experiences, I switched between languages, I broadened my perspective. I lived now within many foreignnesses. To be foreign in my new home was intrinsically unsatisfactory, a concept that wasn't supposed to exist. They threw me out every time they asked that incessant question: where was I from? But in the obvious foreign space of all the countries I travelled through, I was allowed to remain a foreigner. A liberating distance. I would make myself at home in the role for half a day, out of a love of experimentation, not because anyone was expecting me to.

Everywhere I travelled I met immigrants who grumbled about their host country and were looking for the ideal place. It must exist somewhere, they thought. If they expressed envy at how I managed to live so pleasantly at the side of my well-kempt country, I spilled the beans and revealed some embarrassing details about our marriage. When someone started badmouthing this country, calling it one big safe under the main square, stuffed full of stolen gold, a country trapped in its own watertight clock mechanism, not a bit as sweet as its chocolate, I would defend its lovable sides: the rule of law, clarity, perseverance, word and deed as a symbiotic partnership. It took me decades of sailing around the world before I came to recognize these for what they were. And I found this country that much more bearable every time I returned from a trip. The quiet didn't unsettle me like it used to. I would take a deep breath, as though I were slipping back into something familiar, soothing. The country wasn't just self-satisfied, it was self-sufficient, but it no longer annoyed me. Living a comfy, upholstered life meant you could show an interest in the many people in the world whose lives weren't so comfortably padded. An active interest, of course—what else?

Plaid shirt, cropped hair, measured gait? He's got to be a local villager.

I cycle over and stop.

'Where is the parish hall?'

He raises his arms as if surrendering. I was way off the mark. There are immigrants in this village, too. Five minutes later he's walking into the parish hall, where the officer is talking about accelerated integration. He looks at me expectantly, he needs my services. His arrival in the village completes the circle that his ancestor began to draw one hundred and fifty years ago when he moved from here to live three thousand kilometres away. The descendant has with him a family tree and a large photo of one hundred and sixty relatives.

'I've come home,' the resettler solemnly declares.

But when he talks about the chicken farm in the steppe, he comes to life. His feathered minions churned out some two thousand five hundred eggs a day. He was in a managerial position, he stresses, he knows how to work. His current job on the shop floor isn't for him. It's only foreigners working there. They all speak gobbledygook and their willingness to work leaves a lot to be desired.

The way he dissociates himself from other foreigners reminds me that being foreign is itself an identity. He doesn't even have this. He silently shows everyone his family tree. If he sided with the outsiders, they would issue him with a colourful foreigner ID card. But his conceit won't allow it, and his acknowledgement of this would throw a different light on his return. Even with his passport, this languageless man won't find the sense of belonging he's longing for. The officer mentions 'home' and means the country he's arrived from. I'm detached as I interpret, as if I'm impervious to the pain of being deprived of one's citizenship.

After failing with this human route, he looks for an animal way out.

'If I could work with cows, sheep, chickens, pigs, horses, I could easily learn the animal names in your language.'

'It's not just animals you'd have to deal with on the farm,' the officer exclaims, startled. 'The farmers are an uncouth lot.'

The foreign native invites me to his apartment, where all the evidence of successful immigrant prosperity is accumulated in one small space: a black leather three-piece suite facing a *living-room wall lined with computer, television and tea service. Over tea and cheap biscuits, his wife offers me stories from over there, tales of chickens, of early starts, of tough conditions.*

As I leave, she accompanies me to the front door, as the decorum of the steppe dictates, and gets herself worked up.

'When I go out in the street, I hear lots of different languages and see all kinds of exotic people. What are they doing here?'

I get on my bike and hear her as I cycle off.

'There she goes, the foreigner.'

In order to adapt to the new climate, I had to master the experiences of entire generations within a single lifetime, accelerating the evolution of my species. On high alert, I stretched out my antennae and spread my wings to fly. With new capillaries I've built new connections, compensating for the organs and capacities I lacked by flapping wildly. A hybrid creature with a waspish waist, buzzing at high frequencies, with feelers flickering ever faster. In the evenings, exhausted, I would sink into dreams where I'm travelling on trains with a battered old suitcase, and I lose the contents and buy new clothes, or where I'm robbed, and I chase the thieves and beat them up, then make it up with them and they end up giving me new clothes. I'd spend the nights trying on new things, preparing myself for my major transformation. How pointless it would have been to try to force myself into a single, respectable dress when the wardrobes of the world had their doors flung open before me.

I bid farewell to my wishful thinking; no community, no higher being would guide me to where I wanted to be. I learned the alphabet: that action A consequently results in situation B, leaving me with C to reckon with, and that G rarely happens by good grace, and if it does, then I'm not necessarily the beneficiary. I would fall to my knees, begin to crawl, then get up and run, then I'd stumble again but carry on going. I reserved my wishful thinking for when I needed a miracle, and occasionally I dreamt I could fly. I had acquired enough traits to keep me grounded, but not so much that I was weighed down. I rose up, flying high, looking down on landscapes like gardens crisscrossed with toy-train tracks, finally laughing. When I gave up trying to make myself land here no matter the cost, I was floating in a blissful state of limbo. Looking down, I tried to crack the code, to read, not like the locals but between the lines, as I was used to from the dictatorship. No, not everything I'd brought with me had had to be thrown away; I didn't need to start from scratch.

I had a direction now to my tightrope act: uncovering the thinking behind every thought. I had irretrievably lost the familiar wholeness of things but instead I had a new ability to sense a hint of familiarity in so much that was unfamiliar. I decided to cobble together a new dress for myself, one that had never existed before. At that point I hadn't yet realized this was possible, that cultures were coloured fabrics you could haggle over, that I could be a merchant at the bazaar, buying and selling, eyes always open and ruling nothing out. I also had to leave the clan of foreigners behind, to free my thinking. The pure foreignness I then achieved became my familiar refuge; in fact, more than that, it became a choice. I no longer wanted to be without this thought accelerator.

I felt less and less of a hankering for that baroque intimacy with anyone I met, for cosy private conversations populated with chubby words like plump little cherubs. The next time I was informed of something in emaciated, bony words, I endured the brittleness with resilience, not feeling the pain. After all, I had lived in a dungeon before, one that I had constructed from false expectations. Having grown up inside a circle I wasn't ready to appreciate the rectangles and all the geometric diversity. Used to deep red, I shrank away from purple and green. What an animal I had been, reliant on my instinct! Now I've become human, my reflexes are weaker and instead I exercise choice. My heightened senses are at my side, ready to advise; my rational mind coolly learns its role. Somewhere there, between the worlds, is a place for me. It wasn't reserved for me, I've won it the hard way.

I'm no longer plagued by anger and dismay. I'm pragmatic now, a collector, I mix the old with the new, I pick through the flotsam and heaped-up remains. I'll never stop tinkering with my bold construction, which sometimes collapses, sometimes holds up.

I combine smoky emotions from the dirty brown-coal industry with a pristine, biodegradable intellectuality. I'm relaxed as I work, with trained precision, and gradually my vehicle acquires a harmonious, aerodynamic shape. Sometimes I operate this lever, sometimes another, and onwards I drive, always arriving on time. Punctual. And grateful. My foresight and my practical mind are no threat to my open identity, and neither is my gratitude.

The rehabilitation centre is a large building made of glass and wood. The floor of the forecourt is decked with timber like the veranda of a weekend house on a sandy beach. In the entrance hall, plants send delicate offshoots climbing the walls. But the patients here are neither slender nor vertical. The lofty building leaves you feeling airborne, but those for whom it was built can't take advantage of the invitation to lift off. Their bodies are heavy, grounded in wheelchairs. On the first floor under the flat roof, human beings lie horizontal. Here, patients with brain injuries rest in a vegetative state.

'He clenched his fist yesterday,' the mother of the twenty-eight-year-old truck driver excitedly reports.

She and her daughter-in-law travelled a day and a night by bus to be here. They sit there with tear-swollen eyes, working women used to scrimping and grafting, to stay in control of their lives—and their children's—without a husband.

'It's just a reflex, but we will try to develop it into speech,' says the doctor.

'He screamed yesterday. Is that speech?'

'It's an inarticulate sound. The muscles of the vocal cords don't work properly, but it could yet turn into speech. We'll have to listen to him and categorize the sounds.'

'What's the future going to be like?' asks the truck driver's wife. 'We have a baby. He's only one.'

'He won't be able to do his job again. He'll never be quite the same as he was before the collision. But young men can retain vitality despite severe injuries. That's what we're counting on. And we're counting on you, your presence, your mother tongue.'

The wife holds open her hands from which hope has flown. When he got the job as a driver abroad, they made plans and took on debts. She wants to be with him, to take care of him.

The insurance officer talks for a long time about money. The women listen with interest—and with shame. It isn't seemly to expose their misfortune in specific figures. But they fear that the monthly transfers could dry up. The young woman thinks ahead. She has never had insurance to protect her happiness. She learned early on to cope with uncertainty. After the regime change came freedom and hardship. The borders opened, the engineering works in their city closed.

When people conquer their thoughts and feelings, like these two women, they save me the work of creating order when I interpret.

The patient with a brain injury stands, supported by bands fastened around his hips. Being upright instils respect. Then the physiotherapist loosens the bands, carefully lets go of the

patient's head, and the patient slumps down, again a helpless
body mass in a wheelchair. Once a week the young man is
held up for a quarter of an hour, as if to let him sense the goal
that will never be achieved and to feel that past that was taken
for granted.

'How long will he live?'

'Probably decades. He has a young, healthy heart.'

The mother averts her ashen face. It's been said. Spoken
out loud. The physiotherapist carefully stretches the patient's
tense arms, shaves him, brushes his teeth, calls him by his
name. She says she likes him because he's curious. That sounds
strange. But in her day-to-day life it's all about millimetres.
The mother still thinks of the lost whole. The therapist only
knows the wrecked version and keenly notices if a broken part
moves for a fraction of a second. She's a master of the doctrine
of tiny steps. The mother slowly steps on the threshold of the
school of hard knocks.

When I was a child, in our backyard, I was the leader of a
gang that went out doing good deeds. Hardly anyone took us
seriously, but we took ourselves seriously. Secretly, our backyard lived on in me, as a life goal, until finally, far from the
source, it found its form. One evening, a small bus stopped
near me. There was a flyer on the door, showing a man bound
with ropes up to his neck, trying to scream from a mouth
gagged shut. I stepped onto the bus, where they were showing
a video about torture in a far-flung dictatorship, and young

women and men my age were collecting signatures. They seemed attractive, free, peering into the shadows of the world and claiming the right to resistance. I became one of them; I left behind my grief and went out into the world.

Wherever I go, I look for the backyards and find the children—backyard compatriots in spirit and deed. The strong, thin threads that connect me to various groups: these are the backyards where our gang meets, determined to do good deeds. Even if we're not taken seriously by the high and mighty, we take ourselves seriously. And again and again, one of many circles closes, and I know: the curse of exile can be banished. It is possible to turn what you've lost into mobile backyards.

Layer by layer, the cultural experiences are archived in my personality. But they're not just archived, they also chat to each other, and I dare say they've built an airy and resilient foundation by now. It's topped with an empty space, I keep it spick and span. I left the blood ties behind me, but not the concept of kinship. It's constantly expanding, with every transformation. My clothes might change, but I want the feeling of community to stay the same. New identity emerges from transformative action, not just from the enjoyment of a new culture. Not every wolf pack is one I need to belong to.

In one town, I met some peasant women who had been expelled from their villages by the military. The women had been given second-hand clothes by some NGOs. They spoke of how offended they had been by this gesture of weary benevolence. They had lost their homes and were now being expected to forfeit their female second skin—their colourful, home-sewn, traditional clothes. Angry, they wanted to reject this donated foreign identity, but instead they cut the fabrics into strips, squares and triangles, and sewed together these scraps of wool, silk, cotton and lace, to make large, multicoloured blankets to wrap themselves up in. They could accept the warmth of these patchwork blankets they had made themselves, saving themselves while they were on the run. The proud peasant women showed me what a new identity can be. It offers security, but it doesn't lie directly on the skin. We have to cut it up and stitch it back together ourselves. Sewing as an ancient, female communal activity, one that forges identity. Wherever the world grows together, where communities continue to spin their colourful cloaks, I weave my own threads in.

I focus my gaze on the distance, flip my struggle about being foreign on its head and instead demand my right to be foreign, stylizing foreignness as a way of being, always thinking myself into new forms, making myself at home in them. On trains, I befriend people from different cultures. Together we form an entire family. And the rattling train is like a sewing machine stitching together the torn fragments of the world.

Years have passed since I was washed up in the dark onto the riverbanks of this country. I'm getting older and the country is getting younger and more colourful. Together we dine, and I entertain the guests around the table with tales of destinies and fates I have gathered on my travels. To keep an interested audience, I've learned to give them a concise form. Our shared banquet becomes more and more multilingual from year to year. Our foreignness is like the magic porridge pot, its contents bubbling over across the land, spreading across entire continents. But if I look closely, every foreignness is different, and we'll have to find new terms and images: that will be the work of the next generation and the one that follows.

Sometimes I close my eyes and hear languages, a jumble of unintelligible snippets of speech, children's voices, adult laughter. It's bliss to me, just listening, not understanding what they're saying, just knowing that humanity is there, a coincidence of the universe, and I like to listen to its sounds. Exile gave me this radio, I turn the dial. It gets louder and louder and louder.

What is noticeable here is what's missing—no loose objects that patients could use to injure themselves or throw at the psychiatrist's head. The employees carry their keyrings on their hips, they open the doors without warning, and as soon as they're in the room, the key is already turning in the lock again. The windows are jammed so that they only open a crack despite the heat. The closed psychiatric unit looks as if the guards themselves suffer from a fear of open spaces. As if there was a danger hovering above everything that could only be tamed by locked doors and medication. Two kinds of people live here. There is no intermingling between them. Only the healthy have keys, keys to getting well. The only sound is the jingling of the keys, interrupted just by an occasional muffled scream. *This creepy place is where refugees who have resisted deportation are brought.*

The suicide survivor who's been brought in is, in his desire to be dead, the only one with some life in him. He throws his long legs apart, stretches his arms towards the sky, crosses them around his neck, leans forward—stretching movements that here they only allow themselves during exercise. A psychiatrist and a nurse stand there; both men watch the foreigner, motionless. He took liberties without thinking about the consequences: he joined the armed resistance, fathered seven children, and secretly slipped bread to the rebels who came to his village from the mountains. He was denounced, threatened with torture, he sold his house and farm, crossed several countries with his family and asked to be admitted to the local refugee shelter. When the order came to deport them to a third country, the police stormed the shelter. With great presence of mind, he looped his belt around his neck, stuck his tongue out at fate. It worked. The deportation was cancelled, and he was admitted to a psychiatric ward.

'Would you do it again?' asks the psychiatrist.

'Only if I'm deported. Suicide is a sin against God.'

The psychiatrist is a handsome young man in a fitted shirt with shiny snake patterns across the chest. A thick lock of hair falls over his sharply chiselled face, and his hips swing in his tight trousers. Everything about him is mannered, just not his words.

'Do you think you're mentally ill?'

'No, but I'm traumatized by war like all my people.'

'We see no reason to keep you with us.'

The psychiatrist has a merciless expression and rests his chin on his hand like someone looking for love in a gay bar. The suicide doesn't want freedom, the psychiatric clinic is a safe hideout like the inaccessible forest. He is now begging for a certificate for the police, a magic formula confirming his insanity. But the beguiling psychiatrist chases him off his turf without any parting gift.

The fighter launches into a farewell ritual:

'I didn't come to you with the intention of conquering your country, but in friendship. May God repay you. Forgive me if I unintentionally violated your rules.'

These are just clichéd phrases from his culture, but the nurse is touched and ashamed of his inhospitable country, and wishes he could give shelter to the seven children. The psychiatrist stands aloof, cool and elegant. This was a struggle between two men. The macho fighter is in a weak position, tries his hand at playing the victim. After his defeat, he hopes to win me over. I shake him off. He is discharged alone into freedom and danger, into his own life.

How broad I feel during this collision, with one hand reaching this foreign bruiser, the other outstretched to this local gay man, two kinds of outsider and myself a third connecting them. I ping-pong between languages, between cultures, foreignnesses, I catch the balls and pelt them back over the net, rich in experience, fearless, easy, affirming my immigrant fate in all its momentous grace and import. For these newcomers I make available the agility I have acquired, the seasoned veteran *that I am, carrying in every injured cell of my body the advantage of knowledge.*

One day Mara stopped being at my side. She died in a red car that rolled over at high speed. Shards of glass glittered in her blood-smeared hair. The driver, a local poet in a black leather jacket, came away unharmed, and wrote a poem about the beautiful, dead Mara. I inherited Mara's clothes and went to her funeral in her favourite dress.

A mother and her daughter arrived at the refugee camp today. They are about to be questioned. When the interviewer asks about their faith and receives no answer, he looks at me reproachfully as if I'm misinterpreting.

'Everyone has a faith,' he says and turns to the daughter. 'What do you believe in, young lady?'

'A better world.'

'Then you've come to the right place. Welcome!'

✳ ✳ ✳